Thank you?

I'm sure I won't see you around?

Talk about killing a moment. She was ruining everything.

Why couldn't this guy have just fallen asleep and let her escape without a word? Without the rude reminder of her absolute inexperience in matters of casual sex? This wasn't the memory she wanted to take with her. Heat burning her cheeks and that single gruff cough—of whatever awkward response it was—sounding behind her.

Okay, well, no more talk. Even if she'd been doing a passing job of it, a furtive glance at the clock confirmed there wasn't time. She just needed to get her things and go. Quickly.

Halter. Jeans. Panties.

Check, check, check.

Wallet and keys. By the door…where she'd dropped them when they got inside.

For shame, bad girl, she thought with a curling little smile she didn't have the time to indulge in.

MIRA LYN KELLY grew up in the Chicago area and earned her degree in fine arts from Loyola University. She met the love of her life while studying abroad in Rome, Italy, only to discover he'd been living right around the corner from her for the previous two years. Having spent her twenties working and playing in the Windy City, she's now settled with her husband in rural Minnesota, where their four beautiful children provide an excess of action, adventure and entertainment.

With writing as her passion and inspiration striking at the most unpredictable times, Mira can always be found with a notebook at the ready. (More than once the neighbors have caught her, covered in grass clippings, scribbling away atop the compost container!)

When she isn't reading, writing or running to keep up with the kids, she loves watching movies, blabbing with the girls and cooking with her husband and friends. Check out her website, www.miralynkelly.com, for the latest dish!

Other titles by Mira Lyn Kelly available in ebook:

Harlequin Presents® Extra

108—WILD FLING OR A WEDDING RING?
136—FRONT PAGE AFFAIR
171—THE S BEFORE EX

NEVER STAY
PAST MIDNIGHT

MIRA LYN KELLY

~ For One Night Only? ~

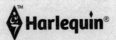

Harlequin®

TORONTO NEW YORK LONDON
AMSTERDAM PARIS SYDNEY HAMBURG
STOCKHOLM ATHENS TOKYO MILAN MADRID
PRAGUE WARSAW BUDAPEST AUCKLAND

Recycling programs
for this product may
not exist in your area.

ISBN-13: 978-0-373-52879-0

NEVER STAY PAST MIDNIGHT

Copyright © 2012 by Mira Lyn Sperl

NEVER STAY
PAST MIDNIGHT

In loving memory of John Morrow

PROLOGUE

SUMMER night, weighted with the heavy thud of bass, poured thick through the converted loft's open windows above. Industrial fans churned overhead, each slow revolution mixing the rhythm-rich, humid air with the heady perfume of bodies in union.

Levi Davis rubbed his jaw against the smooth curve of a toned calf, before easing it off his shoulder to skim down his side in one long, soft, leggy caress. As distractions went, he couldn't have done better than this smoke-eyed, soft laughing, yogilates instructor reveling in a one-night exception to the rules she lived by.

Sexy.

Unexpected.

Elise.

Arching beneath him to graze her teeth over the tendon at his neck, she moaned softly, "You are so wrong for me."

"Completely," he assured with a gruff laugh as he pushed a hank of sweat-damp hair from his brow and rolled to his side. Took in the trim lines of the woman beside him, the silky waves of her hair spilling over his pillow, the smooth limbs tangling in high thread count as she stretched and twisted amid the sheets.

Damn, she'd been exactly what he needed. A full contact, deep impact, whole mind and body diversion from

HeadRush. From the bands and the bars, from walking the rooms and working the customers. From the restless energy that came part and parcel with this leg of the gig. The job was done, the club everything he'd envisioned it could be... The development phase was the fun part for him. Taking his vision and making it real. But once the kinks worked out, Levi was eyeing the calendar, tapping his foot, just waiting for the clock to run down so he could take his profit, blow town, and start again. Unfortunately, a key component to that profit he'd become so accustomed to was a club with a six-month proven track record for pulling a crowd. And he still had a few weeks to go.

So he was stuck.

He'd been stir-crazy. Watching his well-oiled machine run without a hitch. Feeling the press of no pressure around him. The confines of a challenge exhausted.

He'd needed a break to shake it off.

Which was how he'd found her.

Nine-thirty. Both of them walking the aisles of a late-night Chicago bookstore a half-mile away. He'd liked the look of her. So serious, with her nose buried in some beginner's guide to small business. Liked the sound of her even more when his first teasing comment garnered more than a tentative smile. When her nervous fluster gave way to a burgeoning excitement about the studio she planned to open. And then they'd just talked.

He hadn't been after a challenge. Not consciously anyway. But it was *right there*...

He wasn't her type. She didn't do casual. They were incompatible in every way—except the one charging the spaces between their odd topics with an awareness he didn't want to ignore.

As it turned out, Elise was a challenge he couldn't resist. And by the time her breathy "Just tonight" feathered over his lips, he'd been thanking his stars for that.

Levi drew a finger down the tantalizing slope of her shoulder. That alluring combination of good-girl smile and bad-girl bare skin making him want to sink into her again, spend another few hours lost in—

"So, thank you," Elise said, abruptly levering to sit and then looking around as if taking in a scene she didn't quite know what to do with.

Something was off.

"Umm, that was really nice…" She winced a little, hesitated and then reached over to…pat his hand? "And I should get going."

Nice? What the—? Okay. So she was nervous again.

Because she hadn't done this before. Made sense.

And he hadn't been prepared for it…because he hadn't been with someone who hadn't done this before.

"Hey, Elise," he started, reaching out only to have her roll from the bed and start systematically pulling on all the clothing he'd stripped off her less than an hour before. The clothes he hadn't planned on pouring her back into for at least another hour still.

Over her shoulder, she shot him a hesitant glance. "I'm sure I won't see you around, so, good luck with the new club in Seattle."

Levi's brows drew down at the awkward transition. The new and immediate tension radiating from the body that, a moment ago, had been pliant in his arms.

This was a brush-off. Unmistakable in its familiarity, only foreign in that he generally wasn't on the receiving end. It shouldn't matter whether he was the one calling an end to the night's activities. He ought to be grateful there wasn't some uncomfortable scene—okay, a *more* uncomfortable scene—and a slew of misplaced expectations to contend with.

Yeah, he should have been grateful but, watching that tumble of sexy curls spill around her shoulders as she fiddled with the fluttery top she'd been wearing…he wasn't.

Willing her hands steady, Elise Porter tied her halter and dug an elastic out of her jeans pocket. Gathering her hair in a careless wad, she bound it in place, fighting the slow burn of humiliation crawling over her neck.

Thank you?

I'm sure I won't see you around?

Talk about killing a moment. She was ruining everything.

Why couldn't this guy have just collapsed in a heap beside her? Fallen asleep, and let her escape without a word. Without the rude reminder of her absolute inexperience in matters of casual sex?

This wasn't the memory she wanted to take with her. Heat burning over her cheeks and that single gruff cough of—of whatever awkward response it was—sounding behind her.

Okay, well, no more talk. Even if she'd been doing a passing job of it, a furtive glance at the clock confirmed there wasn't time. She just needed to get her things, and go. Quickly.

Halter. Jeans. Panties.

Check, check, check.

Wallet and keys. By the door…where she'd dropped them when they got inside.

For shame, bad girl, she thought with a curling little smile she didn't have the time to indulge in.

But where the heck were her shoes? Searching the floor,

she came to a halt at Levi's bare feet stepping into a pair of faded jeans by the bed.

Oh… "No."

A bark of masculine laugher answered and her gaze shot the length of him—taking in everything from his commando state beneath the low-hung denim, to the hard-cut ridges banding his abdomen, and the wry twist of his mouth and crinkled lines around his eyes.

God, he was good-looking. Too good. She swallowed, turning away before she went all weak-kneed again…and ended up back in the bed she'd just squirmed out of.

"What do you mean *no?*"

"I mean don't get up," she said, an anxious sort of desperation driving her to put some distance between them.

She'd known exactly what she was getting into with Levi when she came back to his apartment. Sex. Simple and straightforward. A good time. The kind she'd read about in magazines and seen on TV. No strings. No repercussions. No expectations she couldn't meet.

It was a one-time, one-night concession granted on the grounds of extenuating chemistry. That and maybe the crazy high she'd been riding since submitting the loan application for the yoga/Pilates studio she and her fellow instructor hoped to open. She'd been ready to burst for hours after leaving the bank—excitement and anticipation thrumming through her veins—with no outlet in sight. So she'd hit the bookstore, intending to brush up on her business know-how, only she'd brushed up against Levi Davis instead.

He'd been gorgeous and funny and so totally, unapologetically everything she'd always stayed away from. But she'd laid the first brick in the foundation of a new life that afternoon. And that night, marking the occasion with one reckless act of indulgence had proved too tempting to resist.

The only thing was, Elise didn't do casual sex. Not that casual even remotely described the kind of carnal intensity she'd experienced in the bed behind her. She made love. Or at least that was what it had been through the two long-term relationships that, until an hour ago, had been the sum total of her sexual experience.

So this was a one-time, magic-ends-at-midnight, exception to a rule—albeit a rule forged more from a lifetime of habit and circumstance than any real moral standpoint, a rule nonetheless. And with mere minutes until twelve—the time she'd *sworn* to herself she'd be gone by—she was in jeopardy of violating the most critical element of the exception.

One night.

That wasn't going to happen.

"I'm going to scoot out of here…just as soon as I find my shoes." Or maybe without the shoes if she didn't find them in the next one-hundred-twenty seconds.

Levi flicked on the bedside lamp, throwing a weak circle of light around them. Scanning the floor, he picked up the duvet piled at the foot of the bed.

"Here we go." He handed over one while considering the other thoughtfully. "It's like a spike heel, a boot, and a sandal all in one."

Yeah, well, that was all well and good, except she didn't really want Levi's take on her shoes or anything else for that matter. No more charm. No more chatter. No more opportunities to taint a memory she fully intended to savor for time eternal with her clumsy replies and awkward talk.

She just wanted out. She needed to go.

Balancing on one foot rather than revisiting the scene

of seduction to sit, Elise hopped about, working the boot onto her foot.

Sweeping his own set of keys off the floor and then grabbing hers, Levi eyed her feet. "Are they comfortable enough to walk in or should we drive?"

Uh-h-h… "You don't need to take me back. Really, I'm good with picking up a cab." HeadRush was right next door and the popular South Loop club had a line of taxis stretching halfway down the block. There wouldn't even be a wait.

"We'll drive, then."

Opening her mouth to protest, she closed it just as quickly beneath the pointed, unyielding stare leveled on her. A reminder of the authoritative edge that had periodically revealed itself through the course of the night. Two hours ago she'd found it dangerously exciting. Attractive. But now—well, fine, she still found it attractive, just not so convenient.

Not when she only had—a quick glance at the clock beside his bed showed the time at eleven fifty-nine. Her heart sank as the numbers flashed to twelve.

Now she'd done it.

Another broken rule.

That would be the last though—and getting in a car with a stranger didn't count, considering she'd already been in his bed. So no more broken rules. No more missteps. Just straight home and a polite goodbye.

Taking a deep breath, she nodded graciously. "Thank you."

It was ten more minutes. Really, what could happen?

CHAPTER ONE

"You did it in a car!"

A week already and still with this.

Elise pushed a windblown curl from her brow and stared, disbelieving, across the hood of the Volvo Wagon at her sister. *"That* is not an explanation for setting me up on a blind date. Which, incidentally, I can't believe you're dropping on me the same hour you stick me with babysitting Bruno, the puppy beast. There's got to be a rule about that or something."

It should have been a perfect day. Following a pre-dawn rain, the sun shone bright against a vivid blue sky dotted with cotton-ball clusters of pure white. It was the first she'd had off in two weeks, and she'd intended to spend at least a piece of it jogging the lakefront paths. She hadn't even made it past Burnham Harbor when her phone rang, and her sister's latest emergency sidelined her at the entrance to Soldiers Field—where she stood now, withering on the receiving end of her sister's caustic glare.

Ally Porter-Davis shook her head, disappointment coloring her words. "A *car,* Elise."

Yes, well, more accurately, she'd done it in a bed. And then a car. And then against the door just inside her apartment. But somehow she didn't think the clarification would win her any points.

"The *car part* was an *accident*."

Ally's brow arched impossibly high. "An accident? Like he, what, just fell in?"

Cheeks flaming, Elise shook her head. "No! Like I wasn't planning for it to happen again…we were at a stoplight and he asked how long I'd lived in the neighborhood and when I looked back at him to answer…" She closed her eyes, awash in the heat of that moment, the look in his eyes when they'd skimmed down her body; the feel of those big hands pulling her over him left her shuddering—

"*That!* Right there." Ally rounded the back end, tapping her fingers against the backseat window as she passed. "That *look* and—and full body meltdown—that's the reason I'm setting you up. You need a man. A relationship with someone nice and reliable. Someone you can *lean* on. Not some thanks-for-the-free-ride-in-my-car guy you're too ashamed to give me the name of either."

"I don't *need* anyone. And, nice try, but I'm not giving you his name because you'd have him Googled and the whole sordid scenario up on Facebook with six of your mommy-and-me *compadres* posting comments in less than an hour's time."

"Excuses." Ally popped the trunk and took a step back as her six-month-old Great Dane bounded free of his confine, spun around with a frighteningly exuberant bark, and then lunged, pinning Elise to the passenger side door. "And about Bruno. Thanks for bailing me out with him. You were the only one I could ask."

The wind knocked effectively from her lungs, Elise stared down at the two saucer-sized puppy paws, planted dead center over her breasts. Shooting an accusing look at her sister, she wheezed, "You are so on my *list*."

Ally waved her off, closing the trunk with her hip. "Your 'So hip-deep in trouble' list?"

For crying out loud. Well, if she broke it down to the acronym, then yeah. This was what happened when people had babies and they struggled with creative ways to stop swearing. "That's the one."

"He's a puppy. You *can't* put him on your *list.*"

As if. Bruno might be the one feeling her up, but it was Ally who'd dropped not one bomb, but two on her today. "I'm not talking about Bruno. I'm talking about you!"

"Me?" Ally spun on her, one hand fisted on her hip, the other swatting at the air in indignant protest. "I'll grant I owe you for dog-sitting like this. But on the date…I'm doing you a favor. That little incident last week was a cry for help if ever I heard one."

This was what she got for confiding.

"It wasn't a cry for anything—" Bruno stomped his big paw with renewed puppy vigor "—aghg, Bruno, no!—least of all matchmaking services."

"Right. You haven't been out on a date since Eric. And that was over a year ago. I've been telling you for months it was time to move on and find someone new, but you keep brushing me off with all the business about not being ready and no time or energy, needing to 'do something' with your life. Blah, blah, blah… And then you go and pick up some random guy—who *does not* count as a date, by the way—and *do it in a car.* I'm sorry, but if that doesn't smack of desperation, I don't know what does."

Elise coughed out her protest. "I am not desperate!"

"Denial, is it? Well, consider this my intervention, sister. Some day you'll thank me."

Some day she'd strangle her.

"I'm not going out with him," Elise said flatly, considering only too late where that kind of statement would take her.

Ally's arms crossed as her upper lip curved into that bossy big-sister sneer. "And I'm not canceling for you."

A battle of wills. The kind that never seemed to end the way she wanted it to.

"Which means, Elise, if you don't show up, then Hank—a nice, emotionally in-touch, stand-up man—will be sitting there Friday night...*waiting*..." Ally's face screwed up into a facsimile of the would-be angst this Hank would suffer "...wondering *why*... Was it something about him...? Maybe he should just stop trying...putting himself out there and *give up*..."

Ugh.

This was why she never won...her sister knew just how to hit her.

Elise let out a long-suffering sigh that Ally batted off like a gnat as she pulled open the rear door of the wagon to check the infant restraints and coo at her groggy son. Straining beneath Bruno's weight, Elise pushed to her toes and craned her neck to catch a peek of that beautiful downy head.

"So sweet," she whispered to her sister, who beamed back appreciatively as she quietly shut the door.

But then Ally was back to business. Hand on hip, stubborn chin leading the helm. "You might like him. Come on, it's a couple of hours. What's the big deal?"

The big deal was Elise didn't want to like this Hank who came so highly recommended. She was afraid to meet some guy who might be perfect, because she wasn't in a place in her life with room for a perfect man.

Her thumb rubbed at the fourth finger of her left hand, and that same twinge of bitterness and sorrow stirred at the feel of the bare skin there.

She simply didn't have enough to give. Not yet. She was starting her own business. Trying to build something, not just for herself, but for all of them. And even once she got it going, she'd probably still need to hang on to one or two of her other jobs. Between that and the situation with her family, she'd be lucky to find herself with five minutes to spare. Let alone the requisite time for phone calls and dates it took to get to know someone.

Whoever this Hank was, he deserved more. Better. "I'm really not interested."

Ally clucked her tongue against the roof of her mouth and shrugged. "But you're going anyway. Later, sis."

Six miles and Levi hadn't found it yet. That quiet numb where thinking shut down and nothing registered but the repetitive slap of his feet hitting pavement. The quiet place where he could mentally disconnect. Recharge. Clear his head. Following the network of intersecting paths at the south end of Grant Park—the grassy lakefront oasis within an urban sprawl, proudly referred to as Chicago's "front yard"—he pushed toward the pedestrian overpass and the far-reaching tracks that ran beneath. Tried to find some sort of Zen place within the gusty wind and rush of traffic, but he couldn't quite get there.

Sweat stung his eyes and oxygen burned through his lungs with each hard pull of breath. Still he kept thinking about the call earlier that morning from his guy in Seattle. Another problem with the contractor. The kind that Levi could have resolved within thirty seconds if he'd been there, but now had them pushed back another day at least.

Turn it off. Turn it off. Turn it off—

"Bruno, heel!" The cry rang out, tugging Levi's consciousness out of that middle space and settling it firmly on a remarkably familiar knot of blonde curls bobbing atop a tight little curvy package of a woman as she stumbled down the path, one arm tethered to a dog almost as big as she was.

Elise. A smile tugged at the corner of his mouth as he followed her with his eyes.

Miss Exceptionally Distracting herself. She'd blown his mind with that crazy, bendy body and those soft, breathy cries at his ear. Her smart-mouthed teasing, nervous fluster, and broken rules.

They'd been good together and he liked her a damned lot. But he had his own rules regarding women like Elise—women who were all about commitment. To their families, their relationships, themselves. He left them alone—and he'd already broken his rules once just to get a taste of her. Only that taste merely whetted his palate for more and it had been a near miracle that he'd finally let her go. Which was why, as much as he might like another foray into the kind of compelling distraction she'd offered, he veered off to the opposite path from the one she occupied. Pushed his thoughts to the rising skyline reaching wide ahead of him. Michigan Avenue…still a good distance from Elise's Printer's Row apartment.

He didn't remember a dog.

That one would have been tough to miss.

Turn it off, turn it off, turn it…

Of course, now that he'd seen her, now that he knew she was right over there, she was back in his mind, daring him to revisit the details of a night he hadn't quite had enough of. Thinking how he'd gotten lost in her body…in her laugh…in that hellfire hot kiss when she'd been pinned against the steering wheel—

Damn. He was watching her again too, jogging backwards like a total jackass. His body reacting in a way that wasn't wholly conducive to running.

He *needed* to run.

Only he didn't really like the look of that Great Dane dragging her down the path.

What was it about these little women with dogs so big they couldn't handle them?

And Elise definitely wasn't handling this one.

The dog bounded right, nearly tripping her. Then cut back left, jerking her forward. Levi's brow drew down as he headed toward the canine fiasco in action. If someone didn't take control, Elise was going to get hurt—

That was when the dog stilled, head snapping around at the sound barely permeating Levi's consciousness.

Fire truck.

The dog took off like a flash, his powerful haunches pushing beyond Elise's strength and taking her down hard into the grass. She bounced once—damn, that couldn't feel good. And whoa, was that mud?—before the leash jerked free of her wrist and then the dog was speeding away even as she scrambled to her knees. *"Bad dog, Bruno!"*

By then, Levi'd already pushed into a dead run. As distractions went, apparently, Elise was the kind that couldn't be ignored.

CHAPTER TWO

HEART racing, Elise shoved up from the wet grass, taking off as soon as she'd found her footing.

Oh, yeah, she got a *list,* all right. And the dog was on it. Just as soon as she got him back.

Only she was losing ground at a rate that didn't bode well for capture. Bruno tore across the open grass, then raced headlong through the "Agora" sculptural installation, giving Elise an instant of relief. Of the one hundred and six nine-foot cast-iron pieces, one of those freaky sets of legs was bound to catch the leash whipping behind Bruno with every wild lope.

Except then he'd broken free and without any signs of slowing. Not even as he closed in on the street…

Oh, God.

The Roosevelt/Michigan Avenue intersection surged with six lanes of downtown city traffic—buses, taxis, and cars, all gunning it to make their turn, catch the light, get where they were going.

She was too far behind.

"Bruno!" she called, panic slamming through her with the knowledge there was no way she could get to him in time.

No. Please don't let this be happening. Please, please, please…

And then, suddenly it wasn't. Two feet from the curb, Bruno wheeled around, jerked back from the street by the man who'd snared his leash at the last second.

"Bruno, heel!" The harsh command boomed with enough force to cow the puppy beast to the ground at his feet.

She couldn't believe it. Bruno was safe. *Saved.* By some stranger she hadn't even seen coming.

"Thank you," Elise wheezed, only her voice came thin through lips that had gone as numb as the legs that had carried her that final distance to where they'd stopped. Dropping into a crouch, she buried her face in Bruno's neck, sucking air in deep gulps until after a minute or two the buzzing in her head subsided and she tried for her voice again. "Thank you... So much... I can't tell you how much I appreciate what you did."

Lifting her face from Bruno's warm fur, she squinted up at her rescuer, who was standing bent over, legs apart, hands on his knees. Breath ripping in and out of him in savage draws. Sweat-soaked hair hung in front of his brow, obscuring his face from view as he gave a short nod of acknowledgment.

Returning her attention to Bruno, she rubbed her fingers through his short hair, each stroke another reassurance that this sweet, sleekly powerful dummy was okay. His tongue spilling out of his giant, toothy mouth, she could swear he was grinning at her.

"Yeah, you're fine," she said, the tremors within her easing. "Which means...you're *so* on my *list.*"

Beside her, her savior chuckled, straightening to his full height. "He's a dog. You can't put him on your *list.*"

That voice. Low, deeply masculine. Distinctive with the kind of roughed-up character a woman didn't forget. Especially when the seductive rumble of it had punctuated the high points of her sexual existence just one week before.

Oh, God, it couldn't be him. And yet that same frisson of awareness she'd felt at the first bookstore bump told her it was. That and the sheer size of him. The man was big enough that before she could make it past his bare chest to his face she had to start again, beginning back at his oversized running shoes, working up the solid cut of his calves to where the powerful slabs of his thighs flexed and bunched beneath his shifting weight.

Wow, he had a lot of leg. A lot of well-muscled, cut-from-stone, chase-down-a-Great-Dane, Clark-Kent-out-for-a-jog leg, braced in one of those uber-masculine stances that somehow combined total fatigue with a readiness to go again. Leg that ended beneath a pair of steel-gray mid-length running shorts that were just the right amount of loose to—

"Elise…you're looking up my shorts."

"What? No," she gasped, shocked. First, in hearing her name, which confirmed her rescuer's identity, and then, because—oh, God—she totally was! Only it wasn't some creepy, salacious leer. Not really. It was just that this was the first time she was seeing the details of the body she'd been wrapped around—had explored with her hands and mouth, had lain awake each night since thinking about—in the light of day. Sure she'd had an idea of what he was built like. Touch was a powerful sense and there'd been enough diffused light from the streetlamps outside for her to see the general dimensions, but this—

Not asking him to leave a lamp on had been a monumental mistake.

That powerful musculature bunched again, showcasing yet another hypnotic set of furrows, planes, and ridges.

Her belly tensed, tightened with the knowledge that *she'd had this*.

Even his knees were nice—

"Yeah," he said with a gruff chuckle. "Except you are. Right now. Still."

Elise slapped her hands over her eyes. "No…well, okay, yes, I was…b-but it's not like you think," she stammered, humiliation—hot and intense—knocking her onto her backside as she grappled for a recovery from what, in that moment, seemed mortification of the unrecoverable variety. "You're just so big and…"

This time his laughter burst out, full and robust. Unrestrained. And the hands she'd only seconds ago dared to release from her eyes instantly clapped over her mouth.

Levi crouched beside her, giving her a square-on look at his face. At the stone-carved cut of his heavy cheekbones, the straight line of his nose, and his squared-off, solid jaw. God, everything about this man said strength. Everything except those deep, whirlpool-blue eyes of his that seemed to warn of danger even as they drew her in with a splash of promised fun.

She'd really hoped never to see him again.

One dark brow cocked to match the smile slanted across his lips, sending a flutter of nervous butterflies batting about within her. "Sweetheart, you just get better and better."

"Uh-h-h…" was all the farther she'd gotten before he wrapped his big hand around her elbow, and tugged her to her feet. Maybe it was the too fast shift to standing or the lingering effects of her adrenaline rush, or maybe it was just the insane reaction of her body and mind being in such close proximity to the best time they'd had in too long to remember, but suddenly her legs weren't quite steady, her knees gone elastic beneath her… And then she was stumbling forward. Straight into the solid wall of hard-packed, hot-to-the-touch, make-her-shiver-and-burn-all-at-once Levi Davis.

"Whoa, you okay?" he asked, the amusement in his tone tinged with concern. His right hand was still closed around her elbow and the left had caught her at the small of her back, holding her in a flush press from thigh to breasts, palms flat against his abdomen, fingertips resting in the shallow well between two tensed muscles.

Eyes straight ahead, staring at the flat masculine nipple mere inches from her face, she managed a slight nod. Blinked and tried to draw a mind-cleansing breath, reminding herself of all the reasons she needed to keep her distance from a man like this…mainly that he was a walking, talking, Bermuda Triangle to good judgment, the pull of him sending her moral compass into a tailspin.

She needed to get a grip. Take a few cleansing breaths to clear her head.

In through the nose—

Oh, *bad idea*. Very bad. This close, all she could smell was the heady scent of clean, masculine exertion.

Sweat.

Soap.

Levi.

God, he smelled so good she nearly groaned. But on the heels of the shorts incident, she'd come across looking like some kind of park-side predator taking advantage of his good Samaritan tendencies to cop a feel and sneak a peek.

She swallowed, trying to ignore the spicy scent of him spurring shadowed memories of his body moving above hers, their limbs a slick tangle, her tongue tracing a salty path up one flexed bicep—

Not helping.

Shake it off, Elise. This man just rescued Bruno. Thank him and step away.

Pushing her gaze upward, she found him staring down at her, the churning depths of his gaze impossible to read.

Or maybe not so impossible after all.

The fingers at her back tensed so the tips pressed into her skin, and the air around them took on the same slow-building charge she'd felt sparking between them that first night. The one that seemed infinitely more dangerous a week past her *one-night's* expiration date.

"Trouble, trouble," he murmured, gaze dropping to her lips.

Trouble. He'd said it just inside her apartment, those hard-hewn features wearing an almost bewildered expression. And then he'd leaned in for one last kiss that had flamed as out of control as the rest of their night.

"Yeah." She let out a shaky breath, taking a deliberate step back. "But I swear, it's only physical."

The corner of Levi's mouth kicked up as he pushed a few fallen strands from his brow. "Thanks. That's a relief. Me too."

"Okay, good." She was sure that was good. And equally sure there was more truth in Levi's words than there had been in her own.

Man, this girl was priceless, but she wasn't getting that dog home alone. All it would take was a pigeon or some stray scrap of trash blowing by and little miss muddy package wouldn't just smear through the grass—she'd be bouncing down East Balboa Street, and Bruno here would be loose for a nasty game of street tag. Neither of which were acceptable. So after a quick check of the time, he said, "Okay, let's head back to your place. But we've got to make it quick. I need to be at the club in about an hour."

Her brow crinkled as she gave him a sort of perturbed once-over, crossed her arms against her chest, and took a small step back. "Levi, I really, *really* appreciate you saving Bruno, and I know I was *looking*...and then with what I said...but I can't have sex with you again."

Sex?

On a day when he hadn't thought he'd even crack a smile, Levi found himself giving into another laugh. Rubbing a hand over his jaw, he shook his head. "I'm offering to help you get the dog home. And so we're clear, I'm offering in spite of the fact that you were looking up my shorts...not because of it."

She blinked at him, shifting her feet. "I swear I wasn't trying to pick you up with that."

"I get it," he said straight-faced, taking up some of the slack on Bruno's leash as she waved in the general direction they were heading. "You just like to look."

"What—no! Excuse me," she huffed, all indignant now. "The shorts thing was—ack, just forget it."

"Mmm-hmm. Whatever." The *shorts thing* was the highlight of his year. And the pretty pink blush burning its way up her cheeks at that moment was coming in for a close second. Especially with the contrasting streaks of mud across her chin and chest, the few blades of grass tucked into the vee of her jogging tank, and the knot of sexy, disheveled gold atop her head. It made her look kind of innocent and dirty all at once.

Not exactly a turn-off.

Not that it mattered.

He'd already decided, no more sex.

"So how are the plans for the studio coming?" he asked, remembering how excited she'd been about it and figuring business talk would keep his head out of places it shouldn't go. "You talk to the salon down the street about the reciprocal discounts?"

The little scowl straining Elise's lips split into a beaming smile as she recounted the conversation she'd had with the salon owner, then she spun into some ideas she'd had about promotions, the neighborhood, and maximizing the space before touching on a few suggestions he'd made the first time they'd talked about her plans. Her enthusiasm was contagious. Attractive. And the more she bubbled on about square footage and curb appeal, the more he had to remind himself he was just getting Elise to her front door. Not pinning her against it to find out just how dirty and wet that slip through the mud had gotten her.

CHAPTER THREE

"YOU'RE telling me Bruno needs a babysitter?"

Rounding the corner of her block, Elise shrugged at Levi's incredulous expression. "I know it's nuts. But what can they do? He chews furniture and apparently he took a half-inch off their back door, digging to get out."

Levi reached down to give Bruno's ears a good rub. "You need some obedience training, my man."

No doubt. "I think my brother-in-law, David, started classes. But then Ally's pregnancy had a few complications, and after that they had a new baby and—Bruno basically got lost in the shuffle. Family chaos. You know how it is."

"Yeah, sure." The flow of conversation between them came to a standstill as Levi studied the old printing houses, the clock tower rising above the historic Dearborn Station.

A few minutes later, they were at her building.

"Well, this is me." She waved a hand toward the front entrance, the motion stalling when she realized how much dried mud covered the back of her arm. Levi was the most gorgeous man she'd ever seen...and *this* was how he'd remember her?

Unfair.

"Thank you for what you did today," she said, then

added an only mildly awkward, "It was nice seeing you again."

His mouth took on that lazy slant that set off yet another batch of butterflies within her. "I'll help you get Bruno inside and then take off."

She nodded a little stiffly, but turned and led the way. It wasn't going to be like before. She was covered in mud and he was just making sure she got Bruno in safely. He'd probably let the dog go at her door and wish her a good life.

Which was completely fine.

Inside the security door, she paused to consider the elevator. Remembered the confines of that space pressing in on them as they'd stood at opposite ends of the car the last time he brought her home. How, by the time they'd gotten off at her floor, the tension between them was snapping taut and it had taken everything they had to make it into her apartment.

"We'll walk up with Bruno," she said, going for a casual tone she didn't quite feel.

"Good idea," he agreed, that knowing smile tingeing the words.

Fine. So what if he did know? It wasn't any secret there was chemistry between them. Or that neither of them were interested in giving in to it again. Definitely not.

Levi blew out a controlled breath. This was worse than the elevator. At least there, he'd been able to watch the floors pass as an attempt at distraction. But here on the stairs, that heart-shaped bottom swinging at eye level less than a handful of steps away had his fingers flexing at his sides. Palms heating at the memory of how she'd fit into them.

What she'd liked.

What more she might—

Not again. He knew too much about her to pretend the

one more time he'd be after to get her out of his system wouldn't be misleading.

So he'd just look.

Let his mind wander with the swing of each step and the tight hug of snug shorts that left next to nothing to the imagination. Damn, he liked those.

At the third floor Elise descended down the hall to her door. She didn't fumble the keys the way she had that first night. But then he wasn't pressed against her back with his mouth on the sweet spot at the curve of her neck either.

Not yet, anyway.

As if sensing the direction of his thoughts, Elise cast a slow glance over the shoulder, the smoke in her eyes swirling thick.

Bruno gave a sharp bark and went for the door, pushing past Elise on his way in. The smoke cleared and she laughed, shaking her head as the dog tore around the couch, his paws skidding out from beneath him at the corner. And then he was lunging for her again, backing her up with the bulk of his weight.

"Down, boy." Bruno dropped to the floor and waited expectantly as Levi crossed to rub his ears.

What was Elise going to do with this dog? "How long have you got him?"

"Maybe another hour, I'm not sure. Just today though." Elise made a move to sit on the love seat across from the door but caught herself even as Levi's hand came up in warning.

"Ugh. Mud." Shaking her head, she peered up at him. "You really think I can't put him on my *list?*"

Levi considered, giving the woman in front of him a thorough once-over.

"Levi!" she laughed in amused accusation, obviously noting where his eyes had lingered.

"Yeah, I've got no problem with Bruno's actions."

A single curl tumbled across her brow. She swept it aside with the back of her hand, leaving another dirty smudge behind. "You like the mud."

The mud. The shorts. The smile. The cut and curves that made up the shape of her. Reaching out, he brushed the spot with his thumb before forcing himself to walk to her door. "Amongst other things. Take care, Elise."

Back against the refrigerator, cordless phone at her ear, Elise strained under the weight of Bruno's bulk. A kitchen chair lay on its side and a three-foot radius around the Pyrex bowl she'd filled was pooled with water. "What do you mean you aren't picking him up?"

"He must have done it before we left to meet you at the park, but David says it looks like Bruno chewed up half of Dexter's toys from the nursery. He's worried it's territorial. That it wouldn't be safe—" Ally's voice trembled between broken gasps "—for him to come home."

One jealous baby chewing up another baby's things. No, this wasn't good.

As if sensing his mommy on the other end of the line, Bruno huffed at the air, his tail wagging hard enough to shake the both of them.

"Ally, okay, take a deep breath."

Her sister made a shaky attempt on the other end of the line. "Elise, I know you're more busy than ever, but all our friends have kids and there's no way I can take him to Mom's."

"No, of course not." They'd always been a dog family, but some overgrown animal thundering through the house and threatening the routine that had become so critical to maintaining the status quo was the last thing any of them needed. Her mom wouldn't admit it, but the situa-

tion at home had been deteriorating for months. Just yesterday, Elise had noticed the lines and shadows around
her mother's eyes had become more prominent. She'd
lost weight. But she wouldn't even consider making any
changes. There was no way Bruno could go there. "I can
handle it, don't worry."

"David mentioned the shelter, but Bruno's not trained.
And he's going to have the stigma of being given up. What
if they can't find anyone to take him? What if they have
to put him—?"

"No. That's not going to happen. Bruno's a good dog."
Sort of. Mostly. "He'll be fine. I'll keep him for now and
we'll find him a nice home with the right people."

Dexter's hungry wail sounded in the background. Ally
sniffed, and Elise heard the shifting of the phone against
her sister's shoulder followed by the soothing hush of a
mother's comfort to her child. Closing her eyes, she let the
sound of it wrap around her heart like a tiny fist.

"You just take care of Dex and don't worry about anything. I'll take care of Bruno. I promise."

"I love you."

"I love you too, Ally."

Eighteen hours later Elise was nursing a new scrape down
the side of her leg, a slamming headache, and a hard grudge
against the Great Dane skidding across her oak floors.
She'd spent the night making calls, seeing if anyone she
knew was interested in a gently used, fixer-upper puppy
beast who didn't answer to her at all, but went by the name
Bruno.

While she'd struck out so far, there were plenty of av-
enues left to investigate. She'd traded her morning classes
to another instructor, but she'd mention him at her classes
that afternoon.

Her anxious gaze landed on Bruno. She just had to get there.

Leaving Bruno in the apartment was unavoidable, so she'd deal with it. Tape some cardboard to the door before she went. Provide an arsenal of chewy toys in the hopes it meant he'd forgo the temptation of her couch leg. Whatever.

It was the *walk* before she left that overwhelmed her.

Staring out the front window at the swath of concrete and obstacle course of signposts, constant traffic, pedestrians, and hydrants, she winced.

David had come over the night before to drop off Bruno's supplies and walk him. This morning she'd braved taking him out herself and barely made it back in one piece. She just hadn't managed to assert her authority in a way that could compete with his brute strength.

She slumped into the couch, trying to ignore the thought that kept creeping into her mind. The obvious…intensely uncomfortable solution to her most immediate problem.

Bruno sat with his big Great Dane thighs sloppy, drooly jowls leaking all over as he stared up at her looking dumb and sweet. He was a big oaf who didn't know any better and needed someone strong enough to show him how to behave.

There wasn't another choice.

Levi shoved back from his desk, eyeing the phone in his hand with slow-rising satisfaction. Elise Porter.

He hadn't even left her apartment before the sud-soaked shower fantasies had begun a relentless assault that, almost a full day later, had yet to cease. It had been a minor miracle he'd made it out of her building at all, and even more so that he'd managed the night without returning to talk her into another bad decision and work his way into her bed.

Just one thing had stopped him.

She'd tried to walk away. At the park and again outside her building.

The chemistry was there. Unmistakably. But she'd resisted it, because she knew—they both knew—he wasn't the kind of guy who could give a woman like her what she needed.

So once he'd gotten her home safe…he'd done the right thing and left.

Only now, she'd called. Reopened a door he'd had one hell of a time forcing himself to close. Which meant all that noble, well-intentioned, do-the-right-thing garbage that had been the source of his sleepless night and his irritatingly, unproductive morning was done.

He eased deeper into his chair, pondering how she'd approach him. Maybe she'd ask for help washing some dirty spot she hadn't been able to reach.

He wished. Connecting the line, he answered, "Levi here."

"Umm, hello, Levi. This is Elise. Elise Porter…from last week at the bookstore…and after…and at the park yesterday…with Bruno…"

Again he was looking at the phone. Okay, so not the smooth approach he'd been anticipating—not that he should have been surprised. And from the sounds of it, she was still going on, trying to cast about more clues for him to nail down her identity.

How many women did she think he picked up during a week? "Elise, I know who you are."

Her breath sounded in rush. "Okay, good. Thank you."

More thanks? She could keep them. He couldn't quite bring himself to accept praise for knowing whose body he'd been buried in a week ago. "Sweetheart, what can I do for you?"

"I know this is going to sound crazy and it's sort of in

violation of the unspoken one-night agreement, but I need a huge favor and you're the only person who can help me."

Levi's head tipped to rest against the leather back of his chair. He couldn't wait to hear this one, especially knowing the kind of tizzy she'd worked herself up to just calling. "What kind of favor are we talking about?"

His mind was already working through a few ideas in explicit detail. And if they were on the same page…he was feeling very generous.

"I've become Bruno's temporary owner, but I still can't quite handle him."

The dog again. Well, he couldn't knock the tactic. It had, after all, worked before.

"You're the only guy I know who doesn't work in the afternoons. I'd like to hire you to walk him today."

Hire him?

Levi sat up in his chair, his mouth twitching against his barely restrained laughter. Damn, she was good. He was no stranger to women looking for excuses to get back within jumping distance of his bed, but, to date, he'd never had one offer cash as an incentive—not that he'd actually take it, but this was too good. "You want to hire me to walk Bruno? How much are we talking?"

Her sigh filtered through the line, heavy with relief. Gratitude. A nice touch. He liked a woman who didn't skimp on the details.

"I was thinking fifteen bucks for thirty minutes at the park."

"No." As a rule, games weren't his thing. But this one was too much fun not to play— And the truth was, he could have really used this call about twelve hours ago. So maybe he wanted to make her squirm a little. "I've already proven I can handle Bruno. Call it an even twenty and I'll run him, too."

That ought to throw a wrench in her plans. No chance of a long intimate talk if he was running down that beast of a dog. Let's see how she wiggled out of this one.

"Deal. That's perfect."

Sure it was. He couldn't wait to see what she came up with next. See if Bruno was there at all. Not that he cared. She'd scored major points for style and originality—despite the sporadic awkward factor he was coming to recognize as pure Elise. So she'd fabricated an excuse to reconnect with him, big deal. Whatever it took for her to make the call, he was on board with one hundred percent, because the fact remained… He just hadn't had enough of her yet.

CHAPTER FOUR

"You're serious?" Levi stared down at the leash, empty newspaper bag and crumpled twenty she'd stuffed in his hand and let out a laugh that was equal parts irritation and incredulous amusement. He should have seen it the second she'd swung open the apartment door, greeting him with that wide, grateful smile. No makeup, her hair stuffed in another one of those elastic things. Ratty jeans and a not too tight T-shirt. "This is *actually* about the dog?"

Elise blanched, her chin pulling back. "You thought it wasn't about the dog?"

What a chump. This was not how it went with him.

He liked to be in control. Hell, he was man enough to know he needed it. And, this thing with Elise. He was most definitely *not in control.*

But, based on the Olympic-level hand-wringing happening in front of him, neither was she.

Rubbing the back of his neck, he shook his head. "Not to sound like an ass here, but it usually isn't. The dog, the lost earring, the house keys—" misplaced thong "—whatever it is, it's usually an excuse."

Shaking her head, she gave him one of those earnest looks that made him wonder how he'd ever gotten past it. Then she swallowed, licking her lips—oh, right, that was how—as she geared up to something big.

"I swear, that wasn't my intention. I mean, yes, I like you."

Ah, hell, he knew where this was going…held up a staying hand, thinking his ego really wasn't up for the speech he'd given too many times to count.

"You're an attractive man and the other night was incredi—"

Her words cut short as Bruno barreled into the room, his huge body skidding into Elise's knees from behind—taking her down over his back.

"Elise—" He was at her side in a second. "Are you hurt?"

"No, no," she grumbled, trying to wave him off even as he caught her.

Fingers moving swiftly, he checked her wrists and elbows, worked his way over her arms…to her shoulders…the slender column of her neck…and the loose, silky spirals falling around it.

Gray eyes fringed with dark ash locked with his.

"I'm fine," she answered quietly, looking away as she pushed to stand. "Getting used to it even."

Right. Following her to his feet, Levi brushed his hands over his thighs in a weak attempt to replace the velvet-soft feel of her beneath them.

Bruno's nails were already clicking frantically over the hardwood as he scrambled to get his lanky legs back under him following a tight turn.

"Sit, Bruno." The dog dropped at his side, his tongue lolling out of his mouth.

Elise ducked to rub a hand over his knobby head. "Good boy. He just doesn't know his own strength yet."

Then after a pause, she shook her head. "Look, this is my fault. I shouldn't have called, but no one else was available. You'd handled him so well at the park, and I really needed—"

Yeah, he got it now. "You really needed help."

Crouching down, he snapped the leash onto Bruno's collar. Leveled the beast with a no-nonsense stare. "You're on my *list,* dog. No more knocking women over."

Bruno met him with woeful eyes even as his puppy feet kept moving. Definitely time to get this dog out.

As he stood, Elise checked her watch, a furrow pulling between her eyes. She walked over to the little catchall table by the door and pulled out a ring with two keys. "These are the spares for downstairs and the front here. I've got to change and leave for my class in about fifteen minutes. Any chance you could let Bruno back in after your walk and then just make sure the door locks behind you after?"

Levi looked at her outstretched hand and back to her face, irritation taking fast hold of him. "Your house keys?"

"You could just leave them on the side table by the door."

Shaking his head, he tamped down the impulse to take her by the shoulders and shake a sense of self-preservation into her. Instead he shoved his fists into his pockets, making it obvious he wasn't taking her keys. "You make a habit of giving these out to strange men?"

Hip cocked, she narrowed her eyes. "Only the ones I've already invited into my body and who rescue me two days in a row."

Invited into her body... Yeah, he'd been there. Was fast on the way to a mental return even as she stared him down. Forcing his jaw to unlock, he blew out a strained breath. "Look, when are you going to be back?"

"About three hours."

That ought to be enough time to get his head screwed

on straight. Especially if he ran for half of it. Looking Elise
over in all her casual disarray, he amended, *Ran hard...
for most of it.* "I'll keep Bruno and we'll meet you back
here then."

Her mind was officially in the gutter. And it was wholly
Levi Davis's fault.

Never, in all her years of yoga and Pilates, had Elise had
the difficulty she'd experienced in maintaining her focus
through her classes today. She'd been an utter charlatan,
preaching that yogic breathing, or *pranayama,* promoted
clarity of mind and balanced emotions, while revitalizing
the entire body.

Ha.

From the minute her hands and knees hit the floor for
Tabletop, through every Forward Extension, Downward
Facing dog, Plow, and Bridge, Levi had been in the studio
with her. A sensual phantom infusing her every stretch
and held position with tantric potential.

By the close of the second session she was about as far
from clarity of mind as she was from purity of thought. It
was bad and she wasn't any better by the time she'd gotten home.

Levi wasn't supposed to want her again.

He was supposed to be the kind of sexy commitment-
phobe she could count on, post one-night, to gently but
firmly maintain an arm's-length distance between them.
Just in case she couldn't quite manage it herself. Not show
up at her apartment ready to play along with whatever ab-
surd scenario she'd concocted to get him there.

Huffing out a breath, she scanned the deserted sidewalk from her perch at the front window. Once they were
in sight she'd jog down to meet them at the street. Thank

Levi and say goodbye. He'd probably want to bring Bruno back inside himself, but that wasn't happening.

The man tempted her in ways she'd never had to ignore before, and, while she wasn't interested in a "real" relationship, she didn't think she could handle the kind of casual on offer.

One more *go*—just for the heck of it—wasn't her style.

And she couldn't really imagine what more would have brought Levi back. Sure, the sex had blown *her* mind, but Levi's experience was vast.

Two hard knocks sounded at the front door. Stumbling back, she hissed at her own stupidity. She'd literally been staring out the window waiting for him…and hadn't seen him coming.

That kind of distraction was dangerous.

Didn't matter. She just wouldn't invite him in.

"One sec, I'm coming." She'd lay it out straight. Apologize for the misunderstanding. Thank him again for helping out. And then a no-touching goodbye.

Swinging the door just wide enough to put herself between the gap, she opened her mouth for the straight talk and no-nonsense dismissal—only to find Levi, propped on one strong arm against the frame, mere inches away. He'd changed out of the track pants and athletic shirt from earlier and into a pale blue oxford open at the neck and rolled at the sleeves, and a pair of worn, asset-hugging jeans like the ones he'd been wearing that first night. His hair was slightly damp, falling in the kind of tumbled half-curls that indicated a quick shower and even quicker towel dry.

Wow, this guy was trouble.

And he wasn't just handing off Bruno's leash.

While she'd been standing there ogling him, Bruno had pushed past her legs and Levi's wide palm covered the curve of her hip as that cocky smile loomed closer.

"How was class?" he asked, those dark eyes intent on hers.

Somewhere in the back of her mind, warning sirens were sounding loud, and yet, when he closed that last distance between them, bringing the mass of his chest into brief brushing contact with hers, she'd long since spent whatever breath it would have cost to protest.

The pressure at her hip guided her back a step, just enough for Levi to continue past her into the apartment.

So much for her plan.

"Kitchen this way?" he called, already halfway down the hall. "Bruno got some water at my place, but we had a pretty good run, so he might need more."

The tap sounded and then a few low-spoken words of praise before her short reprieve was over and Levi was headed back.

Tall. Strong. Overwhelming the narrow width of her hall and sucking the oxygen from the air between them so no breath she took seemed enough to fill her lungs.

Bruno followed him halfway down the hall, before stopping and stretching out on the floor. In the blink of an eye, he fell asleep. It was enough to break that slow-building connection and bring Elise back to the here and now, and Bruno all but collapsing beside her.

Focus shifting between man and beast, she remarked, "I've never seen him conk out like that."

Levi shrugged. "We ran awhile."

Guess so. "Thank you, very much, for helping me out today."

"Yeah, well, I was here." Levi's mouth pulled to the side, wry humor tingeing his words. "And, apparently, you really needed it. So, I'm glad I came."

This was the point to tell him to go. She could see in the slanted gaze he'd fixed on her—he was waiting for it. Only when she opened her mouth to say goodbye, she found herself asking instead, "Why did you come?"

Running a palm over his jaw, he shook his head. Good question.

He didn't like to lead women on, so he'd generally made it a rule to leave one-nighters at one night. But with Elise... it just hadn't been enough. And when she'd provided such a perfect excuse...when he'd seen a way back in without having to think too much about why he wanted to get there...he'd taken it.

"The dog thing." He laughed. "With the offer to pay me. That was...unique." It was also only part of the answer. The rest, he didn't want to examine too closely, but suspected had a lot to do with the way the air seemed to hum with a kind of energy between them.

"The money?" She half gasped, chin pulling back in an expression fast on its way to horror. "You came back because it...*excited* you to be *paid?*"

"What?" Whoa, had that squeak come out of his mouth? And she couldn't really be asking if he— Only the look on her face said that was exactly the conclusion she'd jumped to.

Like that, the humming energy shorted out, leaving a sort of vacuum in its stead.

"Oh, God, were you playing out some kind of a fantasy?" She looked as if she was about to choke, only the damn words just kept coming. "Like you're a gigo—"

"Elise, I'm begging you. Stop." Desperation ran thick through his words. "Just close your mouth before you say another word." Before she ground the last bit of his masculine pride into the hardwood beneath her little bare foot.

She was a verbal train wreck. How could he want her like this?

It was physical. As she'd said in the park.

That crazy, bendy body had gotten under his skin, was all. It couldn't be the twists and turns of her mind getting him so tied up in knots. Half the time it was as if they were speaking different languages. And the other half…hell.

But even with the way her mouth ran when she got nervous, he wanted another night. A whole night. He wanted her to stop spewing ego-shriveling assumptions and get her head back in sync with his.

Her mouth popped open again, making his gut clench. "You should just take the twenty—"

Enough! He'd crossed to her before her next breath, preempting the completion of her thought by catching her around the shoulders and surprising a sharp "Eep!" from her.

"Damn it, it's not the money, Elise." Looking down into those smoked-glass eyes, he searched for that same heat that had been there the first night. Found only confusion. How was he blowing this so badly? "It's just…hell, it's just you. You're different. I don't know what it is. But I haven't been able to stop thinking about you since last week. And seeing you yesterday—" His jaw clenched. "It was all I could do to walk out of here, but I did because I'm just as wrong for you as I was that first night. I've already got one foot out of Illinois, the other one ready to go. I don't have anything *real* to offer you. And whether you want one right now or not, you're still a *real* relationship kind of girl."

He should have left it at that. Said goodbye and gone. Only his hands were already on her, his thumbs brushing over the bare skin of her upper arms, and he knew he wasn't going anywhere. "Aren't you?"

She stared up at him—pupils dark and wide, an erratic flutter at the hollow of her neck—leaning in with each shallow breath. Her gaze dropped to his mouth and the pink tip of her tongue wet her bottom lip.

His heart kicked hard as that connection between them began to untangle. Smooth and pull taut.

Her eyes slid closed. Her next pull of breath drawing him in with it—bringing him closer to those bare naked lips. Parted, ready for him to take—

"I'm seeing someone."

CHAPTER FIVE

LEVI froze a quarter inch from her mouth as something icy cold and distinctly unpleasant slid through his veins.

Not possible. He'd heard wrong.

"What?" He looked up, finding one anxious gray eye fixed on him, the other squinched shut.

"I'm seeing someone. Sort of." Elise let out a tremulous breath, slipping from his hold. "I shouldn't do this. I can't do this."

Because of another man.

Because of the kind of person she was.

He got it. Had understood from the start and known it had to be a fluke to find a woman like her outside a relationship. Figured it was only a matter of time— So what the hell was tightening his tendons and pulling his fingers into fists? Jealousy?

It couldn't be. He didn't get jealous. Ever. And besides, it wasn't as though he had any claim over her. They'd had one night. And an afternoon at the park. Less than a handful of hours combined. She wasn't his...only somehow that handful of hours must have been enough to screw with his head, because even as he closed his eyes to blot that pretty face from his sight, the images of lithe-bodied, little Elise in his bed were brighter than ever.

Hell, he could still feel her wrapped around him. See

the smoke in her eyes thicken as he pushed her closer. Hear his name, all breathy and hot on her lips when she came.

His name.

What the hell was wrong with him?

She wasn't his.

He didn't want her.

No, that wasn't true. He wanted her. *Bad.*

What he didn't want was the complication of what being with her meant. He didn't want her getting the wrong idea about what he had to offer.

But more than any of that…*he didn't want some other guy doing the things to her that Levi couldn't stop thinking about doing himself.*

"Seeing someone, since when?" Any effort to modulate his tone into something casual failed miserably as the words ground out through his clenched teeth.

It had only been a week from that first night, so maybe whoever this chump about to get dumped was hadn't had a chance to make much of a move.

Damn.

It didn't matter. *Right. Keep telling yourself that.*

Elise blinked up at him, those pearly white teeth sinking into her lush bottom lip as if she'd figured out just how very much it was mattering to him at that very second.

"When?" Less gravel and broken glass in that one.

"Tomorrow," she whispered, backing across the room.

Tomorrow?

Elise, Elise, Elise. Not a nice thing to do. And definitely not enough to make him back off. His conscience didn't swing that way.

The corner of his mouth twitched as relief pumped hot and fast through his veins, roaring past his ears, and pushing his feet to move. "How's that work? Exactly?"

"Ally, my sister, set me up on a blind date." She was

watching his every move as he closed in—watching his mouth, his eyes, his chest and, oh, so briefly, lower. "She won't cancel it for me."

Which meant she'd tried to get out of it.

Yeah, that date wasn't happening.

Levi nodded his understanding, doing his best to keep the possessive satisfaction beating its chest under wraps. This guy hadn't even laid eyes on Elise, let alone a finger or anything worse.

And more than that, his little Elise was the kind of sweet thing who didn't want to cheat on a guy she hadn't even met.

They were face-to-face, but it wasn't close enough. Stepping into her space, he crowded her against the back side of the couch, leaning closer still until she'd pushed herself on to the ledge.

A better man might have let her be, given her the space she'd asked for without words. But then a better man probably wouldn't have backed her up there in the first place. A better man wouldn't have wanted to get her off balance and caged in so she had no choice but to reach out and hold onto him.

She could have a better man after he left town.

Reaching for one hand and then the other, he rubbed his thumbs against the pale skin of her wrists, felt the racing of her pulse beneath, and then brought her palms to his chest. "What's she doing setting you up?"

Her gaze was fixed on the spot where her hands rested against him, her breath coming in shallow pants. "It's her version of an intervention because of what happened with you. She thinks I'm…lonely…desperate…something. Doesn't believe me when I tell her I don't have time for a relationship right now. She feels…sort of responsible for me. It's not right, but, whatever. So she called a guy she

knows, a 'nice guy' looking for something serious, to save
me from myself."

Bowing closer, he let his words wash over her temple.
"Do you need saving?"

Her breath caught, but not her hands. Slipping over the
back of the couch, she landed on the seat cushions with
a startled gasp. Only too quickly, she saw her opening
and was on the move. Levi followed her over, hitting the
cushions as Elise slithered to the floor—her slinky, back-
crawling escape making him want to catch her all the more.

Just not quite yet.

Eyes wide, she shook her head. "I don't know what I
need."

Not a problem. "I do."

It was written all over her face—in the spots of color
high on her cheekbones, the smoke swirling in her eyes,
the rise and fall of her chest…and the tight knots of her
nipples pressing through her yoga tank. And if that wasn't
enough, there was that electric current spiking through the
air between them. "And I think maybe you do too."

Oh, God. He was grinning. Not some jovial nonthreat-
ening expression of benevolence and friendship either. Not
even close. This was predatory. Relentless. A warning of
seductive intent that teased her senses toward a heightened
state of awareness.

It made her hot. Scared and excited all at once.

It made her want to get reckless in a way that wasn't
part of her makeup.

"Levi," she pleaded, arms and legs working in a sort of
crablike scuttle to put distance between them. "This can't
be a good idea."

He prowled after her in slow, shoulder rolling pursuit.
Stalking on hands and knees across the hardwood…that seductive gleam in his eyes…the promise of pleasure stretch-

ing in the air between them drawing her toward him even as her hands and feet pushed her away.

"It's not."

No apology. No justification. No reassurance.

"Then why?"

"Because deep down, Elise, I'm not a nice guy." Eyes dark as storm-tossed seas held with hers. "And I want you too much to do the right thing."

A shudder tore through her, halting her retreat as need spilled warm and thick through her belly. "Oh, God, that's good."

To be wanted enough that the right thing didn't matter.

And then she realized: that was how she wanted him.

Waiting, she trembled as Levi closed in—crawling over her until his head was even with hers, his arms braced at either side of her ribs, and one knee was positioned between her legs while the other rested beside her hip.

His mouth curved into a wicked taunt. "Quitter."

"I don't think I want to run from this. From you."

That dark gaze raked over her body beneath his, a breath away from contact. "Don't want a nice guy after all, then?"

She shook her head. Nice guys were overrated. It hurt so much worse when they let you down, because you never saw it coming.

With one arm still braced at her side, Levi wrapped the other around her back. Taking her weight, he closed the distance between them with the hard press of his lips against her own.

Safe in the strength of his hold, she threw her arms around his neck. The demand of his mouth increased, and she opened beneath him. Clung to him as his tongue swept past her lips in a deep, delicious invasion that was all confidence and claim. Nothing tentative, nothing questioning.

Fingers bunched into the fabric of his shirt, she took the

hot thrust of his tongue with a moan, tasted the wet caress of his hunger, and met it with her own.

No one had ever kissed her the way Levi did.

It was all consuming. Possessive. Intense.

And worth anything her conscience had to pay to have it.

Nudging his knee between her legs, he leaned forward, bringing them into closer contact.

Breath ripping from her lungs, she cried out as the thick slab of his muscled thigh flexed against her sex. Satisfaction rumbled from deep in his chest as he palmed the globe of her bottom, angling her hips to meet him again and setting a rhythm of advance and retreat with the rocking of their bodies and wet tangle of their tongues.

Stoking the flame of her desire until it blazed beyond containment.

"Levi," she gasped, the needy ache between her legs spiraling tight through her core as she clutched at his shirt. "Take this off. Please."

Levi shifted onto his knees, pulling her up with him so she straddled his lap. Then grabbing a fistful of shirt from his shoulder, he tugged it over his head and tossed it aside.

Her mouth opened to say…something, beg for more maybe, only the words were beyond her.

He was so incredibly, beautifully built. Broad shoulders. Bronzed skin. And that decadent trail of crisp hair arrowing beneath the fly of his jeans. Hands splaying over the defined contours of his chest, she brushed the tips of her fingers against the tight discs of his masculine nipples, marveling at her own body's clenching response to the grazing touch.

Peering up into his face, she whispered, "What you do to me…"

"Elise. *What I want* to do to you." Catching her jaw in

his palm, he held her gaze. "You sure you understand what you're getting into here?"

The corner of her mouth turned up at his reluctant concession. He didn't want to be a nice guy, but apparently he couldn't help it. "I'm sure."

He nodded, then, leaning back, he dug his phone out of his pocket and held it in front of her. "Call your sister."

Elise blinked up at him, her body a riot of need. "What—now?"

"Now. I'm not above talking you into another mistake, but I'm sure as hell not going to make a cheater out of you while I do it. Dial."

Elise swallowed, thumbing in her sister's number. At the first ring she moved to take the phone from him, but Levi pulled it away, catching her wrists in one hand as she grabbed after it.

"Levi, give me that phone." He had no idea what kind of a mess he could make for her. "I'm serious."

Eyes locked with hers, he held her at bay. "So am I."

Then…

"Hi, Ally, this is Levi, Elise's *boyfriend*…"

Her mouth fell open as the floor dropped out from under her—taking whatever understanding she'd thought she had with it.

"Cancel her date. She's not available."

Levi powered the phone off and then pushed it away, that dark gaze raking down her body to where she straddled his lap and then back up to her mouth hanging in slack-jawed shock.

He didn't mean it. Obviously he didn't mean it.

And she might have confirmed that with him too, if he hadn't pulled her hard against him and taken her lips with a kiss so charged with want, it shorted out all reason and rationale.

CHAPTER SIX

LEVI'S hands tightened at Elise's hip and in her hair as he thrust into her mouth, carrying her half-blind through an apartment he barely knew the layout of.

Her back hit the bedroom door an instant before the door hit the wall behind her, the dull thud echoing around the pants and groans that had followed their desperate flight toward her bed.

She sucked at his tongue and tightened her legs around him, starved for more of the contact she'd never thought to have again.

At the bed, Levi planted a knee on the mattress, easing his hold until she slid down his thigh in a high-friction free fall into need.

Beyond caring about consequences or bad decisions, she bowed forward, licking at his bare chest as she pulled at the buckle of his belt. She wanted him. Inside her. On top of her. All strength and power and masculine need suspended above her as he worked himself in and out of her body.

Fly half-open, Levi pulled a pair of foil packets from his pocket and tossed them to the head of the bed.

He was always prepared. Always thinking, even when she wasn't.

Especially when she wasn't.

And suddenly that seemed like more of a problem than

a relief. Giving in to her body's needs shouldn't mean shutting off her head. Especially since she was perilously close to making a habit of it.

Which brought her back to what Levi had said.

Running her hands up the front of his body, she stilled at his shoulders. "When you asked me if I understood what I was getting into...I thought you meant 'no strings.'"

"Not quite." His mouth slanted in one of those relentlessly bad-boy grins as his hands slid over the contours of her hips, fingers teasing under the hem of her tank, pulling it up until it bunched around her elbows. Eyes burning with appreciation as he studied her pose, arms overhead, half bound by the Lycra top. "Considering the way you've got me tied up, I think a few strings make sense...in the short term."

Her breath hitched, her body clenching in response to his words—though she wasn't certain whether it was the idea of Levi being tied in knots because of her, or the subtle erotic subtext of his statement as it applied to her immediate position.

Before she had time to consider, he'd pulled the tank the rest of the way off and tossed it aside. Set those big hands at her shoulders and gently pressed her back into the mattress so he could go to work peeling her yoga pants and panties free.

Stripped bare, she lay before him, watching the rise and fall of his chest as he surveyed the offering of her body.

Neither of her previous lovers had ever looked at her like this before. As if they'd enjoy spending the entire day just deciding which spot to start with first.

It was arousing beyond expectation to be on the receiving end of that kind of focus. Only the anticipation was beginning to make her squirm.

"Levi." She pushed up to her elbows, peering down the length of her body to where he stood at the end of the bed.

"Damn, I like it when you say my name."

Her brow arched, and she said it again, this time pitching her voice lower as though she were some kind of seductress instead of the mostly awkward, relatively sheltered woman she was.

His mouth slanted further and he reached for her foot. Circled the inside of her ankle with the thick pad of his thumb in a seductive caress that sent currents of electricity racing up her leg. Then carefully he positioned her heel against the comforter several inches to the side.

"Like this."

Her nerves came on line in a flash. It was daylight. The room completely lit from beyond the thin sheer at her window, and Levi had just opened her legs to him in a way that left her totally exposed.

Her bent knee angled in, only his palm was there smoothing over the joint. "You're beautiful, Elise. I've been going nuts thinking about you for a week. Let me see you."

A week. Was it possible? Logic told her no, and yet the stark hunger in those blue eyes told her it was truth. He wanted her as much as she wanted him.

Like this. Right now.

Relaxing into his touch, she closed her eyes. Felt the bed sag and strain beneath Levi's weight and then the graze of his lips at the sensitive skin of her inner knee, the light scrape of new stubble along his jaw, the whisper-soft brush of his hair as he fit the breadth of his shoulders between her legs.

Fists curling into the bedspread beneath her, she moaned at the wet stroke of his tongue teasing close to the juncture of her thighs. "Levi."

Thick fingers wrapped tight around her hip and ribs, reminding her what he'd said about hearing her say his name, and making her throb with the knowledge that she could affect him.

An open-mouthed kiss followed with a pulling suction that had her hips rising from the bed. "Levi, please."

A low seductive laugh sounded as the wet heat of his breath washed over her center. "That's even better. Let's see what this gets me."

"Oh God, Levi!" Her breath burst past her lips with his name—without thought, beyond control—earning another low satisfied growl and a repeat of that incredible crazy thing he'd done with his lips and teeth and tongue.

She started to writhe, felt her body slipping past her grasp, feeding control of itself to the man watching her with hooded eyes as he feasted on her pleasure. Slow licks and soft nibbles, gentle pulls and wicked thrusts had her gasping for breath just beyond reach.

Her fingers had found their way into the thick waves of his hair, and tightened as the tension simmering beneath the surface of her skin ratcheted higher.

"Enough…please." She didn't know how much more she could take.

"Not enough, you aren't finished. I'm going to make you come like this." He licked a slow circle around the aching bundle of nerves before stroking down… "Then I'm going to slide inside you…" thrusting in and out of her with his tongue to punctuate his words "…and make you come again. And again. And again."

"Yes!" Sensation ripped through her center, drawing tight. Tighter. Concentrating into a kind of reverse pressure that built until her body bowed from the bed, suspended for a moment before finally tipping over the edge of desire. Then racing outward until the waves of her release washed through every nerve, cell, and extremity. Body slack and sated, she watched through heavy-lidded eyes as Levi shifted between her legs, kicking off his low-slung jeans. He crawled over her body until his hips rested in the cradle of her thighs, the solid length of him thick and straining against her belly as he reached for the condom above her head.

Their eyes caught and she couldn't help the awed whisper slipping past her lips. "You're amazing."

The muscle in his jaw ticced once, twice, before he covered her mouth with a hot, demanding kiss tasting of her desire and that had her body pulling together once more. He pulled away with a firm shake of his head and a gruff promise. "And I'm not half finished yet."

He couldn't get inside her fast enough. Tasting her satisfaction on his tongue had been a decadent torture. So good and yet painfully not enough. Condom on, he pushed inside her, gritting his teeth against the onslaught of sensation. The stroke of her small heel, high on his back, the tight clasp of her body clenching rhythmically around him, and the breathy relief at his ear when he sank to the hilt.

She'd thought he was after another no-strings night. Not even close.

This wasn't something he was giving up until he split town for good.

Pulling back and thrusting deep, he set a steady rhythm. Watched the tells of Elise's face and body, working her closer to the next rise with each stroke.

She wouldn't regret this. Wouldn't get hurt or form any lasting attachment. She didn't want a commitment any more than he did. But being his beck-and-call girl wasn't going to fly either. So they'd have an affair. A short. Hot. Guilt-free few weeks of fun together.

Arching back, Elise let out a wild cry as her body clenched hard around him.

And he'd blow her mind while they did.

The bed was garbage. Sure, it had held up its end of the bargain, remaining upright when they'd put it through its paces. But barely.

Slitting an eye toward the window at the far side of the room, Levi figured it had to be pushing late evening based on the auburn tint to the sky.

Later than he'd thought. But after burning off a week's worth of bottle-necked sexual frustration he hadn't been fully willing to acknowledge, he'd been wrung out. Add to that, the softness of Elise curled against him—a novelty too tempting to ignore—and he'd slept.

It wasn't that Levi didn't enjoy the feel of a woman in his arms or that, like some guys, he couldn't sleep tangled up with another person. He liked the press of a soft body and deep rhythm of a chest rising and falling with each breath. Liked the pretty scent of a shampoo that wasn't his. What he didn't like were the complications and potential for misunderstanding when he gave into the desire to pull a woman close and just drift off into the night.

Women got ideas when a man held them for too long without trying to get inside them. Ideas he didn't have the time or inclination to dispel.

But with Elise, he didn't have to.

With Elise, the limits on the bounds of this relationship couldn't be more clear. He was leaving in less than two months' time. And she didn't really want him. Well, damn, she wanted him in the make-me-come-six-times-tonight way. Which was about the way he wanted her too. But she didn't want a real relationship getting in the way of her priorities.

Which made this perfect.

Which made her safe.

He wouldn't give her no-strings, because that wasn't what it was. There were strings, but they were uncomplicated.

Him. Her.

A feel-good bit of escape that would last as long as the distraction continued to work for both of them. And then they'd go their separate ways. No hard feelings. No hassle. No heartbreak.

Nothing he had to worry about when he left this city behind.

So he'd indulged in a couple hours of warm-bodied, close-contact shut-eye with Elise.

And hell, he probably would have kept right on sleeping if it hadn't been for the bed and the way it amplified every movement with the supports swaying precariously under the slightest shift in weight.

How this thing had stayed up through what they'd put it through he had no idea.

The tumble of curls tucked beneath his chin shifted, tickling his neck as the body they were attached to wriggled around. He could sense her tension rising and didn't want to give up the comfort that had been between them.

"Thinking about the strings?" he asked into the top of her head.

Elise traced a light pattern over his chest with the tips of her fingers, brushing this way and that. "Probably should have clarified the issue before we…"

The corner of his mouth kicked up as he wondered which words she was trying out in her head.

"Had sex," he offered, chivalrously.

"Yes." Tilting her head back she peered up at him. "What is this? I mean, I don't think I mind, whatever it is. I wanted it—*want* it. But for both our sakes, a little clarification would probably go a long way. This is a… sex thing, right?"

"Obviously the sex is a big part of it, but it's not the only part. Yeah, I can't keep my thoughts out of your panties, but I also just…like you." Levi brushed his thumb over the fine hair at her temple. "Neither one of us is in a place where we can afford a real relationship. I'm leaving and you're working like a dog to make your studio happen. But we've got this connection. Why fight it?"

"So you're my *boyfriend,* but in the loosest sense of the word."

Why didn't he like the sound of that? "How about I'm your boyfriend in the *exclusive,* let's-just-have-a-good-time-while-it-lasts sense of the word?"

Elise's brow lifted with the corner of her mouth, and something inside Levi moved with it. Damn, he liked that smile.

"You really don't want me going out with another guy."

Not even a little bit. "Only child. What can I say? Never learned to share."

The second the words left his mouth he about choked. Beyond the offer of the most cursory information, Levi didn't talk about his life growing up. Hell, he didn't even like to think about it. But that glib remark was just the kind of opening a dedicated family girl like Elise could jump on.

He didn't want her to ask about his family. He didn't want her to know about his mother. He didn't want all those normally innocuous questions that polite people asked giving away the kind of life he'd led. The kind of man he was.

Only she didn't seize the opportunity. A small furrow had dug its way between her eyes, and after a moment she asked, "And you? Will you be exclusive too?"

He didn't blame her for needing to ask. There wasn't any

shortage of available women at his clubs, and nine times out of ten the publicity shots that made the paper pictured him with at least one model-beautiful woman per arm.

But that was PR. Truth was, the club bunnies, while convenient, weren't particularly difficult to resist. Especially the regulars who put in enough hours to know the staff by name, hitting the lulls where they could strike up a conversation while pouring down their drinks.

"I won't go out with any other women."

Elise flopped onto her back, staring up at the ceiling, wearing an amused look of concentration. "So how does it work, then? I call you up when I want…"

Again she seemed at a loss for words, but the devil in him wouldn't help her out of this one.

"…a distraction."

Letting out a bark of laugher, Levi rolled over her and, catching her jaw in the cup of his palm, leaned in for a taste. "That's one way to put it. Or you could say a *date*. *Dinner* maybe? I'm starting to feel cheap."

She coughed a little, that sexy red blazing into her cheeks even as she lay naked beside him. "I—oh, no—I guess I didn't mean— Darn it, stop laughing!"

He wanted to, but for some reason, whenever he was with Elise, he just couldn't.

CHAPTER SEVEN

"Yes, I get that it wasn't much of an introduction to the family," Elise assured, winding her way through the throngs of book lovers populating the annual Printer's Row Lit Fest.

Ally huffed beside her, one hand resting lightly on Dexter's head where it peaked above the front flap of his baby sling. "He hung up on me."

Wrestling against the grin pushing at her lips, Elise offered an acknowledging nod. "Yes."

"*Called me.* And then hung up," she snapped, her diligently nurtured outrage at a high-polished shine. "How did he think I'd feel about that?"

"At the moment, I'm not sure the impression he was making was foremost in his mind."

Stopping at a cozy booth beneath one of the enormous white tents running down the center of Dearborn, Elise scanned the bounty of titles on offer, once again wishing she had more than this single hour to spend at what was essentially the largest free outdoor book fair and literary event in the Midwest. But she had two classes that afternoon, with a few hours of working the club's child daycare in between.

Ally cleared her throat in indication she was waiting for Elise's full attention.

Getting it, she prompted, "He said he was your boy-friend."

Pulling her mouth to the side, Elise wagged her head a bit. "We're exclusive. But the kind of emotional connection and relationship potential you and I would normally associate with that word…it's not really what he had in mind."

Ally's eyes went wide and she gently covered Dexter's tiny pink ears. "You're talking about that full-body melt-down thing again, aren't you? Oh, my God, is this just about sex?"

"No." Elise bristled, even knowing she'd asked the question herself. She thought about the call she'd gotten between classes the day before. Levi inquiring what she was wearing and just how tight it fit in certain places…but then segueing into questions about the various jobs she'd held. Wanting to know which had been the best, the worst, and why. And then he'd had her in stitches as he'd shared the same with her.

It wasn't just sex. Only— "I don't know exactly what it is, Ally. Except it's fun and it feels good and I just couldn't help myself."

Ally cocked her head to the side, affection and concern shining in her eyes. "Be careful. I know you're going into this with your eyes open and all, but this doesn't really sound like you. And I don't want to see you hurt."

Elise shrugged, tamping down any evidence of her own worry. "I seriously doubt I'll have a chance to lose my head. Between our schedules and the probability of the novelty wearing off fast, there just won't be time."

Seemingly satisfied, Ally gave an understanding nod and they moved on to the next booth.

Then, all nonchalance and eagle-eyed, "So you didn't see him yesterday."

"Well, no, I did. But everything just happened the day

before. It was the whole newness thing. I'd be surprised if I saw him again this week."

Elise wasn't going to call.

Fingers drumming the tabletop, she found her gaze once again pulling toward the digital readout over her oven. Eight thirty-six. Two minutes past the last time she'd checked.

Her legs crossed one way.

Then the other.

Picking up her fork, she pushed at the long-cooled vegetables on her plate. Gave up and swept the plate off the table to take to the sink.

She followed the steps of her routine. Washing her dishes. Stacking her plate back in the cabinet. Cleaning the sink and wiping the countertop.

Eight-forty.

Shoot.

She *absolutely* was not going to call Levi. She'd seen him six days in a row since trying to hire him. They'd even worked out a schedule for Bruno. He'd been coming by to pick up the puppy beast before she left for her afternoon classes and then meeting her back afterwards. Spending a few hours making her shiver and moan, and simply reminding her what a spectacular arrangement they had, before heading back to the club for the night and leaving her to either sleep, or, on nights she offered a late class, dropping her off.

But today she'd had to pay back the hours she'd swapped earlier in the week, and hadn't seen Levi at all. He'd picked up Bruno using the spare keys, and kept the beast at his place with the plan to bring him back tomorrow.

Which was fine.

Except apparently her body hadn't gotten the memo and

had been working itself into a heightened state of readiness since almost the moment she woke that morning, thinking about the sound Levi had made when he'd taken her in the shower the day before. That low groan was all hunger and need, and the memory of it had her belly hollowing and her toes curling as a ripple of goose bumps raced across her skin.

This was ridiculous. It was one day.

She could go *one day* without him.

No matter how good he made her feel. No matter how hard he made her—

One day.

It would be easier to get through if she was tired and could just sleep off the rest of the hours.

Only walking past her bedroom door, she found there were two problems with that. The first, she wasn't tired. The second, one glance at that bed and she was thinking about what Levi had done to her the last time they were in it together.

Her breath leaked out on a shaky sigh.

Less than one week, and he'd already made her an addict.

The walls of her apartment seemed to crowd closer as the minutes passed. Her skin felt hotter with every wayward thought, memory, fantasy…all of which seemed to be wrapped around the hard body and intense blue eyes of Levi Davis.

She turned back to the living room, determined to find something on television to get caught up in. It was one day. She could absolutely make it one day.

The live band was one Levi had handpicked, always enjoyed, and brought a huge local following. Hell, like many of the bands he booked, they were already on their way to making the big time…but tonight the hard driving beat reverberating through the floors, walls, and bones in his head was too much.

He was edgy. Irritated. Prowling the club looking for trouble when he'd trained just about every employee too well himself to actually find any. Either that or word had spread like wildfire that he was on the rampage and everyone had wised up enough to make sure he didn't find any slack.

Rounding the center bar, he checked the stock as Finn backed out of his way, quickly moving toward the customers at the opposite side. Trying to look busy. Or, more likely, just busy.

They were low on Grey Goose. Levi raised a hand to get Finn's attention, but lowered it again as one of the barhands jogged up with a full bottle, then took a quick step back when he saw Levi.

Nice. He needed to wipe the scowl off his face and ease up. His people were doing a bang-up job and the fact that it hadn't worked out to hook up with Elise today didn't have anything to do with them.

Truth be told, it shouldn't have mattered a lick to him. It never had before.

He wasn't seventeen, so the driving force below his belt that was hammering his patience into dust didn't make a whole lot of sense.

Par for the course when it came to Elise, it seemed.

No sense in fighting it, making himself and everyone around him miserable. He'd give her a call. Let her know Bruno was all set, getting walked every two hours and enjoying his stint as the HeadRush mascot. He even had a lead on someone who might be interested in taking the dog, so it wasn't as if he was calling just to hear her voice.

Hell no. He had a purpose. And if he happened to want

to know what color her panties were when he got her on the line, then whatever... Or find out if she'd take them off for him if he asked just right... Okay, so maybe he did want to hear her voice. He wanted to hear what she sounded like as he learned just exactly what he could convince her to do with the sound of *his voice* alone.

The phone was out and he'd just finished texting the floor manager that he'd be off for the next thirty or so when he saw her. Little Miss Extraordinary Distraction herself, crossing the dance floor. She moved toward him, the rhythmic swing of her hips, short dress and high heels a seductive call to action.

Damn, she looked good. Almost as good as with the mud.

Sliding the phone back into his trouser pocket, he rounded the open-horseshoe end of the bar to meet her. He leaned close, drawing on that instant spark like a conduit. "Hello, beautiful. Isn't this a nice surprise."

"I hope you don't mind." Her voice barely registered over the noise from the band, so he wrapped a hand around her waist, urging her against him.

"Not at all," he assured, letting his grip tighten the slightest degree. "Can I get you a drink?"

She shook her head, slowly brushing her cheek against his in a sexy, light caress. The contact felt good, only Levi pulled back, wanting to see her. Wanting to witness her reaction to the club he knew she'd never entered before.

His work. His creation.

Only she caught his sleeve and pulled him close again. Slid her hand down his arm and drew his palm to the lower curve of her hip.

His gaze dropped to his fingertips skimming the bottom hem of the simple sheath.

Damn. "What exactly are you up to, Elise?"

She leaned closer so her breath washed over the column of his neck as she answered him. "You look like you could use a distraction."

There was nothing remotely subtle about their exit. Some poor kid in one of those bar uniforms came up with a question just after Elise had pulled the most brazen move of her life, but before the guy even had a chance to speak Levi told him to find the floor manager for whatever he needed. He was taking the night off.

And he'd said it without ever looking away from her eyes.

Now the hand she'd blatantly rubbed over her thigh was locked around her fingers, towing her through the far end of the club toward what appeared to be a service area congested with people. People who wanted Levi.

"Hey, boss—"

"Yo, Levi—"

"Davis, hold up—"

The calls shot out one after another, but Levi didn't break stride or stop for any of them. His only response as they rounded a corner leading to the back stairs was a curt, "Floor manager. I'm off."

Stopping at the base of the stairs, Levi let her pass, resting his hands at her hips as he followed her up.

Anticipation simmered through her veins as she climbed the short flight. With each step, her dress shifted under Levi's palms. Inching up. Sliding down. The silky-soft friction of one sheer layer of fabric coasting over the other in a decadent rush.

At the second floor, Levi stepped close, tightening his grip. The hall was dim, the illumination more blue than bright, with a single door halfway down on the left. Guided by his body against hers, they walked the distance to what turned out to be his office.

Elise entered a room that was more functional than cool, outfitted with an oversized desk, bank of filing cabinets, low-profile table, black leather couch, and a couple of armless chairs that looked as though they'd come from restaurant stock. Like the apartment, there was nothing personal within. But unlike the loft, where the music could only be heard and felt, here she could see everything.

Crossing to the solid wall of smoked glass, she looked down over the main room of the club, the center bar, and the dance floor beyond where bodies moved in union to the heavy beat of the music. "Your club is incredible. You designed all this?"

"Concepts mostly these days. I've got a team working for me, so there's a lot of credit to go around."

"It's wonderful." Then, fingers trailing over the glass, she commented, "I didn't realize there was anything up here."

"It's a combination of mirroring and other effects that basically keep it one way."

Elise shot a glance over her shoulder to watch Levi close and lock the office door. Then test it once.

A smile tipped the corner of her mouth as wet heat licked a teasing path through her center. "One way. So no one can see me here?"

"No one but me."

Levi blanketed her from head to heel as he pressed into her from behind, burrowed his nose into her hair. Starting at her shoulders, he followed the lines of her arms until he caught her wrists in a loose hold, brought them overhead to link around the back of his neck.

"Like this." Warm breath washed over her ear and with it came a low groan of masculine appreciation that sent shivers of excitement shooting the length of her body, tightening her nipples and core.

Again those thick hands skimmed down her arms, following the outer swell of her breasts, drifting in to touch the frame of her pelvis and then down to the tops of her thighs and inward the slightest degree. Her breath caught as he played at the hem of her dress, fingering the bare skin beneath. Making her shiver with anticipation as he toyed with the sensitive flesh still too far from where she wanted him to be.

"Levi." His name slipped out on a soft gasp at another light stroke of his fingertips against her inner thighs, this one higher, deeper.

And then his lips were against the shell of her ear, his breath teasing the whorl. "What did you come here for tonight, Elise?"

Her pulse skipped, though whether it was the question itself, or the light clasp of teeth against her over-sensitized skin, she couldn't know. She loved it that he wanted to hear her say the words, loved that, with him, she wasn't afraid to play this sensual game, or tease a little in return…no matter how far out of her depth she'd found herself.

Closing her eyes, she let the imp in her answer, "I thought we could talk."

"Liar, liar." The low rumble of his claim stroked over her, working her senses into a frenzied pitch.

Her gaze dropped to her dress, riding inches too high against his wrists where his hands dipped beneath. "How do you know?"

She could feel the smile on his lips at her ear as those knowing fingers stroked higher again. Hear the anticipation in the rough scrape of his words against her senses.

"Clubs like HeadRush aren't conducive to intimate conversation. That's not why people come to them. And then—" one finger brushed feather soft against the silk of her panties—the *wet* silk "—there's this."

A shudder ran through her, so intense it nearly buckled her knees. But this was too exciting—too intense to risk that it might stop. So she held strong, silently willing another soft stroke.

"Tell me, beautiful. Tell me what you want before I decide you're going to have to beg to get it."

Her head fell to the side, allowing more access for those warm, wet words to wash over her ear and neck. "Make me."

CHAPTER EIGHT

Elise could feel the muscles behind her clench, the pressure of his palm at her thigh increase for one fleeting, delicious moment, before his quiet curse ground through gritted teeth. Reveling in the tightening strain on the tether of Levi's control, she eased her hips further into his groin and was rewarded with the thick column of his arousal insistent at her lower back.

Heck, she was half ready to beg right now, but she wanted to see what holding back would get her. She wanted to play.

His fingertip followed an erotic trail along the scalloped edge of her panties and then hooked the sodden panel between her legs, giving it a light tug away from her body. Enough that the conditioned air circulating through the office around them washed cool over her hot flesh.

"I want these off."

Oh, God. She wanted them off too. Gone. Savagely torn free by the bite of his teeth.

Or better, ripped from her body by those huge hands. Just the image alone had a quiet cry escaping on her next breath.

Only the hands that worked the panties down were gentle. Slow. Painstakingly careful as they nudged the delicate lingerie past her hips and let it fall to the floor where she gingerly stepped free of it.

Gathering her dress in his fists, Levi drew the garment over her abdomen, ribs, and the rise of her breasts—pausing to abrade the tight buds with a series of slow, soft circles that left her panting, hot and aching, before he worked the sheath to her shoulders.

At his slight nudge she released her hold around his neck and let him strip her completely.

She was bare. Completely exposed. Standing in Levi's office, surrounded by a building full of employees and masses of club-goers who had no idea they were even there. It was the most provocative thing she'd ever done.

The car didn't count. That had been an act of desperation. But this, this was conscious thought pushing her to dive headfirst into Levi's pool of hedonistic pleasure.

When Levi's hands returned, there was nothing between them and the bare skin of her body. He covered her breasts, taking the achy press of her nipples against his palms. Coasted lower to what she was beginning to recognize as his favorite hold at her hips, and pulled her back into contact with the steely ridge that fit snug against her behind, and the powerful slabs of his thighs and bulk of his chest.

One hand splayed wide and hot across her belly. The other resumed the downward trek to her sex, covering her there.

And then, with the nudge of his knee between her legs, Levi widened her stance and pressed a single finger between the parting flesh beneath.

"God, you're wet," he whispered into the hair behind her ear.

Her heart skipped as the anticipation built with his provocative words. His deliberately too light touch offering only enough contact to drive the breath from her lungs on a shuddering gasp and make her wonder if her knees could hold her, before she realized she didn't care. "Oh, God, please. Levi."

It shouldn't have been possible to hear that satisfied twist of lips in his breath, but somehow she did.

"Mmm, that's close, beautiful. But I want more."

That soft sliding finger trailed another teasing path through her wetness, ever so lightly circling the tight bundle of nerves that threatened to make her Levi's slave. He would come so close—only to veer away. She needed more.

Her hips began to move with his punishing caress, seeking more—though whether it was more contact or more of the sweet torture driving her wild she didn't know. All she knew was no man had ever held her at the brink the way Levi did. No man had ever dragged her to the heights he took her, carried her beyond where she thought possible to go, and then taken her even further. No man had built her desire to such a peak that she believed nothing could surpass the pleasure derived from the journey alone—and then proved her so completely wrong. Giving her a climax so intense she didn't just feel as though *she* had shattered, but the world around her had shattered as well.

That was where he was taking her now.

That was why she would wait as long as she could. Resist with everything she had. And draw out every single minute of the pleasure Levi offered her.

Her fingers slipped free of each other and wound into the short silk of Levi's hair, eliciting a low groan of approval as his mouth opened over that tender spot where shoulder joined with neck—and he sucked.

Sensation shot the length of her, coiled round her womb and cinched tight just as he pushed his finger, thick and long, inside her.

"Levi," she gasped, bucking against the long-awaited invasion, rocking in time with the slow thrusts, trying to take him deeper, trying to take what she'd only moments before been working to hold off. "I need…oh, God…I want…"

"Tell me. Is this what you need?" he asked in a taunt that told her he knew exactly what she needed. That this was all part of the game.

"Yes…more." The answer was half plea and half cry, and was rewarded with the thick penetration of his fingers, stretching her in decadent pleasure. Ratcheting her tension higher until she bowed taut. Making her blind with longing until her throat worked convulsively as she swallowed back the sobs that threatened to break free with his every controlled thrust. Until restraint and control and resistance were crushed beneath desire.

She cried out, a desperate keening sound that found its beginning and end in a place within her she hadn't known existed. And once tapped gave forth a font of pleas that voiced her every soul-deep need.

The angle of Levi's thrust shifted, the heel of his hand making sweet contact with the spread of her feminine flesh and that single needy place. The air in the room, in her lungs, in the world around them seemed to collapse into the gravitational epicenter of her body, hold for an instant that rolled over with the weight of forever before releasing, surging outward and pushing sensation to the very extremities of her being. Overloading her nerve endings, filling her so past what she believed her capacity for pleasure to be, she thought she might burst.

Welcomed it.

Wave after wave washed over her, threatening to drown her in a bliss too deep, too wild and too far-reaching to find her way back from. But then Levi was there with her. His powerful arm braced across her torso, holding her tight to him when she didn't have the strength to stand on her own.

Sucking great draws of air, she tried to find her place in the universe once again. The world spun as Levi turned her in his arms. Opening her eyes, she found him looking down at her, his features taut with barely restrained yearning, and she couldn't breathe at all.

"That was…" he shook his head, his voice rasping gravel rough over nerves still overcharged and sizzling "…the sexiest thing I've ever seen."

If she hadn't been staring into his eyes, if the truth of his words hadn't been blazing in their blue depths, she wouldn't have believed it.

A man like him. A woman like her.

It shouldn't be possible, but in that moment it was.

She wanted to tell him it was him—that no one had ever made her feel the way he did. But before she could open her mouth, find the voice that she feared she'd left in the ether, rough hands lifted her atop the desk. Levi reached over his shoulder and, grabbing a handful of his shirt, tore it over his head even as his other hand made short work of his belt and fly.

"And I want to see it again."

CHAPTER NINE

"ALL I'm saying is that it's cliché. Not that it wasn't good."

Reclined against the black leather sofa in his office, Levi chuckled and looked down to where Elise lay on top of him, her stubborn little chin stacked on her hands over his chest. "It can't be cliché if it was an emergency."

One slender brow pushed up into an amused arch. "An emergency? How exactly was that?"

Catching one of those soft loops falling about her face, Levi twisted it round his finger before letting it spring free into its silky coil. "You needed a distraction. And I needed to hear you moan. The office was the closest place to make it happen."

"Your apartment is next door. Literally attached to the club."

"Too far." And it had been. The moment Levi had seen her walking toward him, he'd been ready to strip that dress off her and put her up on the bar. Only he wasn't a public display kind of guy and the chest-beating beast in him was typically of the mind that if Elise went the rest of her life without letting another man see that unbelievable expression of ecstasy on her face, it would be okay with him.

Hell, he couldn't even think about her soft parting lips and half-lidded eyes without his groin starting to tighten.

Elise was giggling at his more-than-honest response.

That lithe little body of hers moving in a way he couldn't ignore. And then she let out a soft sigh and something inside his chest tightened too.

So different.

Her lips drifted over the spot and she kissed him there. Softly. And if he hadn't liked the feel of it so damn much, he would have flipped her beneath him right then.

"Besides," he added, "Bruno's over there. You know as well as I do, if we'd gone through that door, we'd have been looking at a walk before we got anywhere near the bed. Plus the guys downstairs would be pissed if I threw off the rotation."

"The rotation?"

"Yeah, they like walking him. Worked out some kind of system for who gets to do it when."

A second passed and then another.

"Levi, you're not what—" Swallowing once, she shook her head, then turned so her sexy mess of hair concealed her face and prevented him from seeing her eyes. It wasn't the sort of thing he'd normally care about—maybe it wasn't something he'd even notice—but right now he was curious what she'd been about to say.

Gathering a bit of her hair, he was about to tuck it aside when she shifted above him and then began backing off the couch. "I should get out of here."

Levi's brows pulled down as he pushed to his elbows. She wasn't looking at him as she slipped her dress over her head and let it slither down her naked body.

"It's getting late and I have to work early."

Right. It made perfect sense. And maybe the only reason it didn't feel that way was because he was an arrogant S.O.B. and he hadn't been the one to suggest it. Maybe he just didn't like that Elise kept getting the jump on him…

even when the out she offered was the one he'd always taken in the past.

Levi swung his feet to the floor and started pulling on his own clothing.

Or maybe what he didn't like was the way that easy connection between them had evaporated between one breath and the next, and now Elise looked as if she couldn't get away fast enough. As if they'd completed the sex portion of the program and, uncertain about what came after, she was ready to bolt.

He could tell her to stay. Wake up with her in his bed. Have her again and then drive her back in the morning.

Instead, he reached over and tugged her closer so she stood between his knees and he could rest his hands at the backs of her thighs. "I'm glad you came tonight."

Light fingers trailed down his chest. "I was worried about interrupting you at work. I won't make a habit of it."

"Stop by any time you can."

Elise wasn't the type to show up at four in the afternoon and stick around until closing, sucking back drinks and getting stupid. Hell, she barely drank at all—which was one of the reasons he could actually relax around her. There wasn't any gauging reactions and weighing responses. No questioning judgment or keeping an eye on her for her own good. He didn't have to work when they were together and he liked that.

"Won't I get in the way?"

Maybe if he were at the start of his project, rather than the end. But the truth was, HeadRush and its staff were virtually running without him. "No. Besides, everyone needs a break once in a while, right?"

She met his eyes. "I needed a break like you. Like this."

Yeah, so maybe he'd needed it too. His palms coasted up her legs beneath her dress to— "No panties."

Even in the dim light, he could see the blush rise to her cheeks. "I haven't found them yet."

"Is that so?" A quick glance across the office and he located the scrap of silk in a little heap against the base of his desk. Urging her closer, until her shins met the front of the couch, and then further still so all she could do was let out that soft breathy laugh and crawl back onto his lap— her knees straddling his hips as they sank into the leather cushions—he shook his head. "I don't think it would be right to let you leave until we found them."

"Oh, really?"

Really. He settled back into the cushions, pushed the bunched fabric of her dress even higher than it had ridden on its own. Ground his molars down. "Don't worry. I have a plan."

She arched that sexy brow at him, silently telling him she couldn't wait to hear this.

"We'll check the couch here first. Thoroughly. Then have a look around my apartment."

"Your apartment, hmm. What about Bruno?" she asked, that sinful smile doing things to him that suggested the trip to his loft was a ways off.

"We'll walk him first and then resume the search. I've got a good feeling about the bed. But if we don't find anything…you'll just have to stay the night."

CHAPTER TEN

LEANING against the concrete pillar just outside the studio, Levi offered another acknowledging nod to the women clearing out of Elise's class.

Shortly Elise herself exited with another woman, presumably the owner, who hung back to lock up.

"I wasn't expecting you guys," she said, jogging over with a wide grin.

"Yeah, well, Bruno was getting all riled up. So I thought we'd just swing by and walk back with you. Grab some Thai from that place on the corner."

Elise reached down to rub Bruno's knobby head. "That would be great. I picked up a late shift at the coffee house this evening, but I've still got a couple hours before I need to be there and I'm starved from skipping lunch."

Over the past week, he'd been surprised by the complexity and extent of Elise's schedule, and that for the first time in his adult life, he was the one doing the accommodating. He'd known she taught classes throughout the day at a couple of Chicago's upscale fitness clubs and local studios, but the peripheral jobs she held to boost her income had been a surprise. Her odd shifts at a trendy coffee place and waiting tables one night a week meant she was pulling somewhere in the neighborhood of sixty plus hours, most days starting as early as five for the before-work crowd and, on waiting-tables night, finishing after midnight. She was relentless.

But the faint shadows around her eyes suggested she wasn't tireless. And experience told him that once the contracts got signed, she wouldn't be slowing down any time soon. Not if she was anything like him.

He respected the hell out of the way she was going after her goals. Giving them everything she had. It was the same way he went after what he wanted. But he couldn't help wonder if her body could take what she was demanding of it.

She'd assured him her classes were varied and broken up throughout the day, and that she spent more time correcting form and posture for her students than actually holding the poses herself, but even so— "You shouldn't skip meals, the way you work."

"I know. And normally I don't, but today I had to run over to a property with Sandy and I didn't have time."

Sandy, the partner fronting the other half of the cash they needed for the space and equipment. "I thought you had a place?"

Elise glanced off to the side for a moment in a way that made him think the meeting hadn't gone the way she'd hoped.

"She's having second thoughts about the location and wanted to look at something different."

When she told him the address, he ran a hand over the back of his neck. He knew the neighborhoods pretty well from when he'd been scouting locations for HeadRush and the one she'd mentioned landed only a few rungs above barren wasteland…and nowhere near up-and-coming. There wasn't much in the way of pedestrian traffic. It was cheap—industrial space going for probably a quarter of what they'd have to pay for retail—but it wasn't the kind of spot Elise had been talking about.

As if reading his mind, Elise glanced back at him. "We talked about the money up front. About what kind of place we wanted to open." Blowing out a frustrated breath, she met his eyes. "Our business plan is based on projections from an area like this one. It's based on that location specifically. We'd have to withdraw our loan application and resubmit with a new plan. New numbers. More waiting. But I don't know if I'm even interested in what she's suggesting."

"So what did she have to say about it?" He would have liked to have been there. He could read investors like a book. Ten minutes with this Sandy and he would have known exactly what the situation was.

"She keeps coming back to the money." After a deep breath, she shook her head and stared off into the sky. "I'm worried. We've been talking about this for so long and now that we're finally moving forward, I've let myself—"

"What? Get your hopes up? That's good, it's how you should be. And maybe she's just got cold feet. It happens, especially with first timers, and often they get past it. Give her a call tomorrow and talk to her. Tonight just try not to worry about it."

With a tight nod, she agreed. But by the time they'd reached the restaurant, she hadn't relaxed. "I hate to do this, but would you understand if I asked for a rain check on dinner?"

She wanted to go over the business plan. That was what he'd want to do if it were him. Hell, that was what he wanted to do right now—so the solution seemed simple enough. "How about you pick out something to eat from the menu here and then we'll head back to your place? If you like, I'll stick around and we can talk it through. If you'd rather be alone, at least you'll have food."

Soft gray eyes blinked up at him, too grateful for what he'd offered. "You really wouldn't mind?"

Not when she looked at him like that. Hell, no, he didn't mind.

Ninety minutes later, the cold remains of their Shu Mai, Kee Mow, and Pad Thai littered the far end of the small kitchen table where they'd set up Elise's laptop and the files she'd put together on her plan for the studio. Levi had sorted through the details asking questions here, offering an opinion there, and in between reminding her to eat.

Now, leaning back in her chair, she watched as he closed the laptop and eyed her across the open cardboard containers. "I could talk to Sandy with you."

"No. Thank you, but I'd like to talk to her myself. After this—" she waved her hand between them "—I feel more confident with what I want to say."

That and she didn't want to risk Sandy feeling ganged up on. Levi could be intimidating when something threatened not to go his way.

Levi pushed back from the table and started closing the flaps on the various carryout containers. "Not sure I really helped that much. I'm impressed with the business plan you've submitted. I'm sure the bank will be too."

Elise walked around to the fridge to put away the leftovers he handed her. "You helped. I put a lot of work into gathering the information we'd need, but I just don't have the experience behind me to know if I'm missing something vital. So another set of eyes makes a huge difference to me."

Then, propping a hip against the sink, she swallowed past the unexpected well of emotion. "I need this. I need it for myself."

Levi set down the silverware and, wiping his hands on a dishcloth, reached for her. Took her fingers in that loose grasp and rubbed a thumb over her knuckles. "Tell me why?"

She wanted him to understand. Only when she opened her mouth to explain, she didn't think she could.

As if sensing her hesitance, he leaned back just far enough to give her a bit of that devastating smile that flirted with her will. "Okay, how about we start small? Why yoga and Pilates? How'd you get into that?"

Easy enough. "I'd been taking classes with my girl-friends back in college. It started out socially, just some-thing we did together, but when I realized how it cleared my head and strengthened my body, I was hooked."

"College?" Levi looked past her and she could almost see the wheels turning in his head. The facts flipping through his consciousness. She'd told him she didn't have a degree.

"I only got three terms in."

"What happened?"

And that was where it got sticky.

"My parents had some…financial issues. And the money we'd thought we'd have for my education, wasn't there. It wasn't their fault," she added quickly, hating the conclusions Levi might jump to. "It wasn't anyone's. Just how it worked out."

Levi gave her a moment to elaborate, and, when she didn't, simply took her answer at face value and moved on. "Did you like school—while you were there?"

She thought back to that first terrifying day, when she'd been so filled with nerves and apprehension she'd begged her dad to take her home. He'd walked beside her, prom-ising that he and her mom were only a short drive away—that they'd always be there for her—but she needed to stay.

Joking until she'd relaxed enough to put her fears behind her. She'd never doubted him.

And then there'd been the late-night study groups, the quad, her dorm and her friends. All that excitement and intensity around a future that was theirs for the making. Even now she felt the surge of it like an echo inside her.

So much had changed. So fast.

"Yes, I did." She shrugged, because, really, what more was there to do? "But we were going to lose the house."

It was only half the story. And that Levi wanted to press was evident in the faint lines between his brows, but she knew right now he wouldn't. So with a simple shake of her head she went on. "Ally only had one semester left and a job lined up for when she was done— It just made sense for her to finish. My parents needed my help and I wanted to stay close…but I needed an income too. Something *flexible*. Which made me think of the yoga and the offer I'd had from one of the instructors to pick up a class. Well, that's what I ended up doing. Along with a lot of other odd jobs. But the yoga stuck. I enjoyed it. My classes got more popular and pretty soon I had full load."

"Had you chosen a major yet?"

"Business," she offered with a little smile.

Levi nodded back to the files on the table. "You've got a head for it."

"I guess that's something we'll just have to wait and see about. But I hope so." Looking down to where their hands met, she thought about what there was between them. It was uncomplicated. Honest. Easy. Good. She could talk to him. She could tell him the rest. Maybe even tell him what was happening now—only there was a sort of freedom in his not knowing what she wasn't prepared to give up. When they were together, she could forget. And so for now, half the story was all she wanted to give.

"I'd like to finish that degree some day. But until then, this studio is everything. Life isn't perfect. It never will be. But I just want something that's mine. Something I can commit to. Invest myself in and watch grow. God, I just want this to work so much."

Levi pulled her into his chest, stroking a hand down her back. "You've made a good start, sweetheart."

Drawing a slow breath, Elise melted into all the warmth and strength surrounding her.

She felt so good within his arms.

So safe and secure.

This was what Ally always talked about, she realized. Having someone to lean on. Someone there to just hold her when she needed a little extra support.

That was all that was happening, though. It was gratitude and a kind of empathetic understanding flowing between them, not some misplaced emotional connection. Levi knew what it was like to be starting out. He was offering his experience and support, because, no matter what he thought, he really was a good guy. Just not the kind of good guy she was going to keep.

But so long as she kept what they were doing and where they were going straight, she could enjoy this and no one would get hurt.

CHAPTER ELEVEN

"I'M JUST saying, it's weird, is all." Ally folded a few slices of turkey onto a small wheat roll, covered them with a layer of bib lettuce and glanced over her shoulder. "I mean, I get not wanting to abuse Levi—your *boyfriend,* who hung up in my ear—with a bunch of forced proximity to the fam… but is *meeting* him really too much to ask?"

Playing with Dexter's feet as he lounged down the length of her thighs, his heavy lids creeping closer to closed with each breath, Elise shook her head, answering in a quiet singsong voice. "Don't try to work me over, Ally. I'm not going to give."

A plate with the sandwich, a few baby carrots and a pickle spear slid in front of her. "It's not like I'm asking for his social security number. I just want to meet the guy. Lay eyes on him so I know he's on the up-and-up."

"No." Keeping her eyes on Dex, Elise gathered his slumpy body and handed him off to his waiting mommy.

"Down we go, little man. Mobile time." Ally deposited him on his back in the small bassinet beside the kitchen table, tucked a light blanket over his chest and stroked his fuzzy head.

Returning to her seat, she leaned on one arm, stretching over the table. "When you keep me in the dark like this, my mind starts to wander. Wondering why? I'm thinking drug addict, ex-con, grifter—"

"Grifter? As in con man?" Elise laughed, picking up a baby carrot. "Nice try, but, seriously, you know exactly who he is and what he does. His clubs make the entertainment news enough that he's practically a public figure."

"That's what he does, Elise. Not who he is." The cajoling, half-teasing tone was gone as her sister looked her straight in the eye. "We've always talked to each other. Been there for each other, when no one else could understand what we were going through. The stuff with Mom and Dad—no one got that but you and I. Not David. Not Eric. It's always been you and me. But with Levi, you tell me less and less every time I see you. What gives?"

"It's not that I'm trying to exclude you." She shifted, uneasy with what wasn't exactly the truth. "I'm just trying to figure a few things out."

"Like where the relationship is going?" Ally asked, her tone pitching toward hopeful. "Because it's more serious than you thought?"

No and yes. She knew exactly where the relationship was heading. Straight for a dead end. But it *was* more serious than what she'd planned.

They'd spent every night together for a week now. And the night before, when she'd been waiting for him to finish at HeadRush, all she'd been thinking was how good it would feel *to sleep* with his arms around her. *Sleep!*

So wrong.

She'd known from almost the start, this wasn't *just* sex. What she hadn't been prepared for was just how much more it would be…to her. And to try and explain that to someone else, when she didn't even want to admit it to herself—no.

This thing with Levi was…different. But he was exactly what she needed—what she wanted, right now. She just couldn't let the emotions that were ready to run get away from her.

Still, Ally didn't deserve to be shut out. Fortunately, she had a bone to throw. "I'll tell you this. Levi thinks he's got someone who wants Bruno. We're meeting him this Saturday."

Ally's eyes lit up, welled around the edges as she reached out and grabbed Elise's hand. "Really? Do you know anything about him?"

"He likes to run. Lives about an hour out of the city—"

"Wait." The hand gripping hers squeezed tight. "This isn't like you telling me that Bruno's going to live 'on a farm' or something, is it?"

Elise shook her head, laughing at a typical Ally response. "No, I swear. Levi said he's an older guy...early fifties maybe. Divorced. He works from home and had a Great Dane that died this past year. He'd been waiting to get a new one, but thinks he's ready now."

"Oh, my God, he sounds perfect!"

Elise's heart swelled at the memory of Levi sweeping her around in a half circle and laying that triumphant kiss on her before telling her about his busboy's dad, and the whys and why-nots of the people he'd talked to about Bruno already and how this guy seemed to be the best fit. "I know. I couldn't believe he'd been looking for someone like that."

The corner of Ally's mouth shifted up in line with her brow. "I wasn't talking about Levi...but knowing you think he's perfect might be enough to satisfy my curiosity about the guy. At least for another day or so."

Elise's throat went tight and dry, choking back the denial surging within her. Only even if she'd been able to force the words free, what would it get her? Her sister wondering why the heck she'd be trying to convince her Levi wasn't perfect...or if Elise might be trying to convince *herself.*

* * *

"You going to be on your best behavior, boy?"

Levi crouched in front of Bruno, nose to nose, rubbing the short hair of the canine's neck as he gave him a little man-to-man.

Bruno huffed at the air, his back paws shifting over and again.

"Yeah, you're going to be good."

Elise watched the exchange, uncomfortable with the way her heart kept doing that little flipping business and her arm kept moving as though to reach out for Levi.

"You going to be okay?" she asked, trailing her fingertips across one strong shoulder.

Levi glanced back at her, braced his palms on his thighs and pushed himself to stand. "He'll be fine."

Elise cocked her head at him, noting how, even now, Levi was rubbing his hand over Bruno's knobby head. "I meant you."

That gruff laugh and wry smile were pulling at her again. Making her want to step into his arms and soak up his warmth.

Instead, she turned away. Walked the few feet down the paved path by Museum Campus, watching the waves of Lake Michigan while she tried to put her head back on straight. She wasn't supposed to like him this much. She wasn't supposed to get attached. And yet, how could she fight it when every time an opportunity arose—and half the time one hadn't—Levi was there, showing her what a wonderful guy he was. Tempting her to imagine him in all the places she'd thought he'd never fit.

Down a ways, two little boys lined up by the water fountain. One trying to boost the other up to reach it, but not nearly big enough to do so. A couple stood a few paces off, hands linked together, matching smiles stretched across their faces. After watching a handful of unsuccessful attempts, the man dropped a kiss at the woman's temple and stepped in, sweeping the boys into one arm each to hold them up for their drinks.

A family.

To have one of her own had been her dream. For the longest time, if anyone asked her what she wanted from life…the scene playing out across the park would have been a piece of it.

She'd had the chance to make it happen with Eric. But the timing hadn't been right and, when faced with what it would cost her, she hadn't been willing to make the sacrifice.

"You can't ask me to choose."

"And you can't ask me to spend my life coming in second place in yours. If you love me, you'll come with me… you'll pick us."

Levi's wide hand wrapped over shoulder, drawing her back a step into the solid strength of his hold. His breath teased into her hair.

"What are you thinking about?"

What another man who'd been leaving had offered her. Something she'd been telling herself for the last year she didn't want—didn't have time for—but seemed to be thinking about more and more over the past two weeks regardless.

Pulling out of Levi's grasp, she smoothed a smile into place and turned to face him. "Nothing. Doesn't matter."

Levi's brow drew down, his mouth firming into a flat line as those deep blue eyes tried to probe the thoughts she didn't want him to see.

A hoarse call of Levi's name had his attention reluctantly shifting over her shoulder. Tightening the leash looped around his wrist, he stroked Bruno's head with his free hand. "This is it, boy. Whole new life ahead of you."

* * *

The exchange hadn't taken long. It was clear from the minute Bruno and his new owner laid eyes on each other, they were going to hit it off just fine. A half-hour later Levi and Elise were walking back to her place alone.

She'd seemed withdrawn afterwards. Her arms wrapped tight around herself and Levi'd experienced the unpleasant sensation of Elise shutting him out. Though it drove him nuts that she didn't want to talk to him, he understood how hard saying goodbye to Bruno had been. And unfortunately there was nothing he could do to fix it. Short of going out and buying her a new puppy, that was—which didn't make a whole lot of sense considering the whole point had been to get rid of this one.

Regardless of the attachment they might have had to him, neither he nor Elise was ready to be a full-time dog owner.

Sure, he hadn't exactly looked forward to giving Bruno up, but once he'd done it that same sort of freeing relief washed over him he experienced every time he signed the papers handing off one of his clubs or turned in the keys to the place he'd been living or put another state line behind him.

A weight lifting. A bind loosening.

Maybe one he hadn't even registered…yet. Eventually he would have though. He always did. And then whatever comfort he'd been taking from whatever it was he'd been trying to hold on to would start to suffocate him like a blanket he couldn't kick loose.

That was just the way he was.

Slanting a glance to Elise walking beside him, he knew it would be the same with her. Yeah, she'd affected him differently than the other women he'd known. Because she *was different*. In a million ways…so many he hadn't even begun to figure them all out yet. And that had to be part of it. This crazy pull between them.

He hadn't exhausted the challenge. Hadn't unraveled the mystery.

Elise was constantly giving him something new to work out. Keeping him on his toes. And putting him on his knees.

But eventually the challenge or whatever it was that kept him coming back for more would fade, and he'd *need* to walk away from her—whether there was a convenient excuse like moving out of state to start the next job, or not.

Which was why, when it was time to leave, he'd go, packaging his goodbye within the neat confines of this temporary affair they were both prepared to have end.

Until then…

He reached for Elise, tucking her beneath his arm as they walked. Offering her whatever comfort she'd take from his just being with her.

CHAPTER TWELVE

BACK stiff and feet aching, Elise untied her black barista apron and tucked it under the pick-up counter. Sagging against the sink with a wan smile, she counted her tips. Thought again about finding a second job that paid better and then reminded herself that the flexibility was the primary reason she worked this one. And really, the tips weren't that bad. They served food all day and the Dearborn Park patrons were a generous lot, with a good turnover. Besides, it was walking distance from her place. Which meant she wasn't blowing coin on transportation to work there.

Definitely a benefit.

Normally the energy of the popular coffeehouse was enough to get her through a shift, even after working five to two at the athletic club, but today the cacophony of whistling steam, clanking ceramic, and shouted orders had grated from the moment she'd walked through the door.

The situation at home was deteriorating.

Ally had mentioned it the week before, but, being a bit of an alarmist, her street credit wasn't what it could be. Elise figured her sister was making more of a missed call or off day than she should. But when Elise had dropped by with groceries the evening before, she'd been greeted at the front step with a tentative smile and news that it wasn't a good day. That a visit would be too disrupting and they'd talk on the phone later.

Of course it wasn't the first time a bad day had kept them from seeing each other. It was just that Ally had met with a similar response two days before. And when Elise had talked to her mom this morning, all of her questions had been shut down with the most minimal response and her mother had asked her not to come to the house for a few days.

An anxious knot tightened Elise's stomach.

It wasn't as though her mom weren't entitled to her space or privacy. It was just that she'd been systematically shutting herself off from the world for nearly six years... and she needed a life. If she wouldn't even let her daughters in—

"Elise?"

Jerking upright, she scanned the crowd of customers. Caught on the man in the twill shirt and khakis, cleaning his glasses on the end of his tie in front of her. Sandy hair, clipped neat. Handsome in a lanky sort of way.

Oh, God, not now.

"Eric?"

Her thumb moved to that touch point at the base of her fourth finger.

This was the last thing she needed today. *He* was the last person she wanted to see.

"I know. Surprise, surprise. I didn't realize you'd started working here," he said, taking in the coffee shop with a subtly disapproving stare that gave her the impression he was revisiting the conversation from a lifetime ago when he'd told her to quit working. That, married to him, she wouldn't need a job.

What a mistake that would have been.

"Finally get over the whole yoga thing?"

She bristled at his easy dismissal of her dream, but then pushed it down, reminding herself that she was already on edge. And Eric hadn't done anything to put her there. No doubt he was as uncomfortable seeing her as she was him, and was simply struggling for something to say.

Still, she hadn't expected to see him.

"What are you doing here?" she asked, digging deep to find a smile that matched her civil tone.

At the cheeky toast of his whipped mocha, she nodded, smiling a bit. "In town, I mean."

"I told you I'd be back," he said, eyes trained steadily on hers as if to gauge her reaction. Her remorse maybe. "That it probably wouldn't be more than a year and a half. Turns out it was less. The transfer went through last week."

He must have worked himself to the bone—but he looked good for it.

"Congratulations, Eric. You earned it." Finding she truly meant it, she added a sincere, "I'm happy for you."

He waited a beat. Stepped closer. "You could have been happy *with me,* Elise."

Then, shaking his head with a wry smile, he asked, "How have you been? How's your dad—your family?"

She swallowed, taken aback by the bold statement and the questions in the warm brown eyes that had never truly held her. And she realized he was wrong. She wouldn't have been happy with him. Not the way people committing to a life together were supposed to be. Their relationship had been nice. Pleasant. Convenient.

Tepid.

They'd gotten along.

Shared interests.

Enjoyed the other's company.

But never had there been even a fraction of the intensity she experienced with Levi. This man had been her friend.

And the reason his forcing her to choose between moving for his career and staying near her family had been so crushing was that it had felt like a betrayal from someone who should have understood.

So they'd both made the right decision. Marriage would have been a terrible mistake.

"I've been good, Eric. Busy. I'm trying to open my own studio, so I'm working even more than before, if you can believe it."

That chagrined expression said he could.

Skimming over the details of her parents, she filled Eric in on her family. Primarily, the adventures of Ally pregnant, and the joy of her new nephew Dexter. When she'd finished, she found Eric watching her with something that might have been pity in his eyes.

Something she didn't like. Crossing her arms, she took a step back.

"Sounds like the life we'd always talked about. Only it's someone else's."

Deflated, she shook her head. "I just want different things these days. A studio of my own. Working toward that goal has taken up most of my time."

"Sounds lonely."

Lately it hadn't felt that way. But once Levi left…

Eric set his mug on the counter between them. "Just take care of yourself, Elise. I want you to be happy. I want you to have the life we couldn't have together."

Something was going on with Elise.

Levi'd seen it the second she stepped into his loft. Sensed the tension and noted the way her smile didn't match her eyes. All kinds of alarms had started sounding in his head as he braced for something he wasn't going to want to hear. Something he wasn't going to let happen. But then she'd walked up to him and, without a word, gone to work on his belt.

Not him.

Whatever it was. It wasn't about him.

And that should have been enough—with any other woman it would have been. But this was Elise.

Stilling her hands at his belt, he lifted her face with a finger beneath her chin. "What's going on?"

She blinked, as though surprised—frustrated that he'd noticed. Or frustrated that she'd *let* him notice.

"Talk to me. Maybe I can help."

Levi waited for her to explain, but instead Elise stared down at the floor. "No. It's been one of those days. At the coffee shop—no, before that…"

"Hey, come here." He pulled her into his arms, drawing in the sweet scent of her shampoo, subtly overlaid with roasted grounds.

"I should have canceled… I just thought if I saw you tonight—"

She broke off with a weary shake of her head that made the center of his chest ache as if he'd taken a blow to it. "What did you think?"

"That you'd distract me. Do what you always do and make me forget about everything else." With each word, her eyes darkened like a swollen rain cloud about to burst. "Just for a few hours."

"That's what you want? Me to make you forget?" He would have liked her to confide in him. To share her burden, but maybe the distance she kept was smarter than this playacting at intimacy he couldn't seem to resist.

"It was stupid—"

Catching the soft curve of her cheek in his palm, Levi tipped her face to meet his. Gave in to a single second of wondering how this woman had the ability to affect him so completely differently than any woman he'd met before. And then pushed every ounce of his cocky arrogance to the fore as he intentionally crowded into her space.

"What, you don't think I can do it?" Fingers trailing lightly up her hip, waist, and ribs to graze the outer swell of her breast, he lowered his voice to a slow, seductive taunt and spoke against the soft shell of her ear. "Guess I've got something to prove, then."

"Come on. You need to eat." Levi laid the boxes of pasta all'arrabbiata, fresh baked bread, and insalata caprese across the foot of the bed as Elise curled her legs beneath her at the center.

"I know. I just lose track when there are too many things on my mind."

Forking up a spicy penne, Levi pulled a distraught frown. "Are you telling me I didn't distract you enough?"

Hand up to him, she clutched the sheet to her chest, laughing. "I'm distracted! I swear."

So distracted, it was a miracle she was sitting upright and not sleeping in a boneless heap of sated exhaustion.

"Yeah, well, just in case—" He rounded the bed, coming to sit behind her as he held the pasta to her mouth, waiting for her to bite.

Delicious.

"Let's talk about your favorite subject. The studio. Do you want to tell me about the wood you think would be best in the studios or the quotes you got on the Pilates machines? I'm game, either way."

A weight lifted as she drifted toward the comfort of her fantasies and plans—the productive escape she used to shut out all the things beyond her control.

Even Levi saw that she'd turned talk about the club into some kind of security blanket.

"I don't know." She shook her head, wondering again what she would do if the studio plans fell through. She'd put everything into this one, abstract idea.

Her breath came short. "Oh, God, what if the loan doesn't go through?"

Fingertips trailed down her spine and then the flat of his heel rubbed low across her back. "It will. Don't worry."

"It's just that I can't even imagine what I'm going to do if it doesn't." Peering over her shoulder at Levi stretched across the bed, she confessed, "I haven't got another plan. I mean, it's not as though I won't have work. But there's no next step. No fallback plan. I've put everything into this studio and suddenly I feel like if it doesn't go through, I'm going to be left with nothing."

Suddenly *nothing* held a whole new meaning for her. When things had ended with Eric she'd been upset. She'd felt abandoned. But even just twelve months ago things had been different with her parents than they were now— she'd looked into her father's eyes and, once in a while, she'd still seen him looking back. Today, even her mother was shutting her out.

And then there was Levi. She'd never shared a connection with anyone like this before. Whether it was one-sided or completely skewed the scales in balance didn't matter. She finally knew what it was to have someone who made her feel whole. Someone who added colors to the world she'd never seen before. Losing that, she suspected, was going to be worse than if she'd never had it at all.

And without the studio to distract her—

"No," Levi said, cutting into her spiraling thoughts. "If it doesn't go through you modify your plan and try something else."

"There you go again. Always with the straightforward simple solution." Her eyes heavied as the slow rub of his hands over her muscles calmed the tension within her. "What am I going to do when you're gone?"

The words drifted past her lips without thought, riding on a soft sigh that ended as abruptly as the calming strokes that spurred them. It was the first time she'd said anything like that. The first time she'd acknowledged that she'd begun to rely on him. And she'd done it aloud.

Strong hands wrapped around her hips and towed her across the mattress and into Levi's lap. Two shifts and she was laid back, held in the crook of one strong arm, while the other braced on the bed across her torso—the position somehow making her feel both protected and vulnerable all at once.

"So maybe you need a backup plan. Let's start one." Thick hanks of hair hung over Levi's brow, darkening his eyes as they bored into hers. "What if you came with me?"

The words seemed to eat up all the air between them, making her "What?" come out in a wheeze that sounded far more desperate than it should have.

"If the loan doesn't go through, why not come up to Seattle with me for a while? We'll work on a new business plan together." The corner of his mouth eased into that cocky grin. "As it happens, I have a knack for that sort of thing. I'm familiar with the neighborhoods you've been looking at around here. We could fly back a couple of times to work out the details. Meanwhile, you could see SoundWave coming together. The grand opening will knock your socks off."

She had no doubt. Especially considering she was stunned to the point of being blown over already.

He wasn't supposed to ask her to go.

Granted, what he was talking about was temporary. Nothing more than an extension to their affair with the added bonus of access to his business savvy. Only she still couldn't get enough air in her lungs and started to shimmy out of his hold. "A new business plan?"

Levi followed her out of the bed. "It'd be a few months. We're having fun, so why not?"

Why not? Why not? Why not?

It was like a cruel joke without a punch line.

A million reasons. All flashing through her mind in the faces she loved too much to abandon.

"I can't. My family is here." And even if she wasn't leaving for good, a few months was too long to risk being gone. Too much could happen in that time and what if they needed her? This week with her mom alone demonstrated just how quickly things could change. No. She couldn't leave.

"Besides—" she pushed all the confidence she could muster into her voice "—the loan's going to go through, right?"

"Right." That cocky smile closed in on her and then Levi pressed a quick, hard kiss to her lips before striding from the room.

She'd blown him off, *thank God.*

Heart slamming in his chest, fists locked around the edges of the porcelain sink, Levi stared hard into the bathroom mirror.

What in the hell had he been doing, suggesting Elise come to Seattle? It made no sense. Her life was here. Firmly and solidly rooted in all the things she'd never give up. And he was a rolling stone. Practiced in kicking off the moss that amounted to a superficial collection of employees, acquaintances, and belongings accumulated during the development of each club.

It was what he did.

He moved on. Alone.

So what was he doing asking Elise to come with him?

Sure, it wasn't as if he'd been proposing. He'd basically invited her to a two-month, off-site tutorial on how to set up a new business—and only if her current plans fell through. He cared about her, of course. She was a sweet girl with ambitions he could respect and a struggle he could relate to. So he'd offered some help, figuring it would give them both time to get their fill of whatever it was between them.

He hadn't been trying to keep her.

Never expected her to agree.

Truth be told, the fact that Elise turned him down flat made her all the more appealing. He hadn't thought it possible, but she wanted even less from this relationship than he did.

Perfect.

Man, he was a head case.

Pushing back from the too intense guy in the mirror, Levi shook off the tension from his close call. Ignored the nagging tug at his gut and the faintly bitter taste of something he couldn't quite swallow in his throat.

Maybe tomorrow he'd ease back some with Elise. Only as he swung open the door and caught sight of the bare length of skin exposed as she leaned over the pasta—the tentative smile that seemed to stretch wider with his own— he forgot about any plan he had beyond being with her.

CHAPTER THIRTEEN

RESTLESS beneath a cover of thin cotton, Elise followed the streak of late-night headlights as they stole through the slats in the blinds and cut a path across her bedroom ceiling.

Though Seattle hadn't come up once in the week since Levi mentioned it, the moment was never far from her mind.

He hadn't been pressing for a commitment. She knew that.

Levi had been clear about the temporary nature of the invitation extended. That all he was talking about was a couple of months. A little more fun.

Except Elise couldn't stop reading it as more than that. She couldn't stop her thoughts at the point where Levi told her they'd play a little longer before he sent her packing back home with a shiny new plan for a future that would take place in a different state than the one where he resided. No, she couldn't leave well enough alone. She'd had to take it a step further…to the fact they shouldn't have been anything but a single night. But already it had been a month and still Levi didn't think he was going to be ready to give her up by the time he needed to leave. He'd reconsidered his plans, *again*.

Queasy nerves stirred her belly and Elise rolled to her side, tucking her knees up close.

Now Levi was suggesting—albeit, only as an alternative if her loan was denied—they turn the single month that remained into another three? What then?

Nothing was as set in stone as she'd believed entering the relationship. Levi had destroyed the security she'd had in knowing that, no matter how much she'd begun to care for him, there were those hard and fast rules, inflexible boundaries that kept her from getting in too deep. From finding herself in another position where she had to choose.

By changing the rules, he'd given her license to envision possibilities she never would have before. Scenarios that revolved around forbidden words like *somehow, what if,* and *just maybe.* Words that dared her to hope and all but promised heartbreak.

The phone beside her bed flashed bright with a text alert and her belly did a little flip, her body coming alive as all the doubts and worries weighing on her evaporated into thin air. *"You awake?"*

She dialed him back. "It's two in the morning. Of course I'm awake."

A gruff laugh answered, then, "Hmm, so not sleeping… but tell me you're already in bed."

"I am," she murmured, adjusting the pillow behind her head. "Where are you?"

"In my car. I was on my way home and thought I'd swing by if you were up."

This time it was Elise laughing. "On your way home? Considering the only thing between your club and apartment is a layer of concrete and some insulation, I'm wondering how you found yourself in the car."

"Call it a *driving urge*…but enough about that. What are you wearing?"

Her thighs shifted together in a sensual rub that was all about anticipation and the low, gravel-rough sound of Levi's voice. "Why do you want to know?"

"Because I've got about five minutes until I get there and I'm about to give you some very detailed, very specific instructions. Timing is everything."

Elise smiled, her eyes drifting closed. "In that case, I'm not wearing anything at all."

Hours later Levi woke alone in Elise's bed, that sleepy contentment he always felt waking there crumbling at the sound of a muffled voice down the hall. Following it, he stopped at the front room.

Elise stood with her back to him, phone at her ear. Spine rigid beneath her thin robe. The tension radiating off her hit him before her words. "How long?" Then, "No, I'm not ready. Give me ten minutes…I'll call you back."

"Everything okay?" he asked when she'd disconnected the call and begun pulling on her jeans without her underwear. He was a dog for noticing when something was clearly wrong, but he was also a guy. And guys didn't miss that kind of thing.

Unwilling to look at him, she nodded once. "That was Ally. There's a…situation. I've got to take off. I'm sorry, but you should probably go home. I'll talk to you tomorrow."

"There's a situation. At four in the morning. And you think I should just take off?" Crossing to her, he caught her chin in his palm, forced her to face him and saw the shadows in her eyes. Shadows he'd only glimpsed in her most unguarded moments. The ones he'd wondered about, but were gone so quickly, he'd always just let pass. But not tonight. "There's no way I'm leaving without finding out what's going on."

And short of some husband she'd forgotten to mention being on his way home, he wasn't leaving then. Okay, chances were good he wouldn't leave regardless.

Her chin took on a stubborn set and he wondered if she'd refuse him flat. Tell him to take a leap. Only beneath that stubborn jut broke the barest tremor. A crack in the façade she was trying to maintain.

Pulling her into his chest, he ran a hand over the tumble of curls that framed her face against his pillow like a wild halo. He'd half expected her to pull away, but her hands crept up between them and her forehead pressed against the center of his chest.

Whatever this was, it was bad. He didn't know what was wrong. He just knew that in that moment she needed him.

Drawing a shaky breath, she took a step back, quickly arranging the features of her face to disguise the pull of fear and sorrow it was too late to hide. "It's my dad. He's… missing."

Everything inside Levi came to a grinding halt. Missing.

Immediately Levi started flipping through the details he knew about her father…found his scowl deepening as he came up blank. Which didn't seem possible. The way he knew Elise—the way she talked to him for hours at a stretch about her dreams for the studio, about books and movies, about local politics and pop culture, about her sister's family…

But not her parents.

Parents, family and home life were subjects Levi was a master of avoiding. But until that very minute, he hadn't realized how easy Elise had made it. Because she'd been avoiding them too.

Sure, there'd been a handful of stories from her youth. All white-picket perfection. A few more from high school. But nothing current. And yet he hadn't even noticed.

Which took skill. The kind gained through practice.

Suddenly the ground beneath him felt loose and ready to give.

What was she trying to hide?

As he stared into the troubled eyes of a woman he cared too much about, ugly scenarios he didn't want to consider rose to the surface of his consciousness.

"Heaven help us, Elise, tell me what's going on."

Elise swallowed, nervously checking the phone still clutched in her palm. "My father was diagnosed six years ago with Alzheimer's. He doesn't work, and my mother takes care of him at home." After a breath, she turned to him, her eyes brimming with helpless tears. "Tonight she woke up and he was gone. The car and keys are still there, and so are his shoes. My mom's got to stay at the house in case he comes back. She's the only one who might be able to calm him down. They've already called the police and David's driving around, but Ally's home with Dex, and he needs another set of eyes."

Levi nodded, the well of relief within him nearly enough to bring him to his knees. Alzheimer's was a tragedy. And he pitied Elise's entire family for the toll it had taken on their lives. But the scenarios he'd begun to imagine… had been much, much worse. What was wrong with Elise wasn't about some seedy secret. It wasn't a trip down a bottle-littered memory lane. And it wasn't anything he could fix. But a missing parent was something he understood all too well.

"Okay, sweetheart. Call Ally back. Here's what we're going to do…"

An hour later, they were working their way through the grid of neighborhoods surrounding Elise's parents' home. Levi driving as Elise scanned the alleyways, sidewalks and gaps between parked cars. Ally riding with David, while one of Levi's HeadRush managers, who happened to have six younger siblings, stayed with Dexter.

Elise stared out the window, eyes searching. "I didn't mean to lie to you."

Levi shot her a questioning glance.

"About my family being so great. You said they sounded perfect, and I told you they were because that's how it used to be. And sometimes, maybe, I'd just rather pretend it still was."

Levi watched the road. Taking in her admission and turning it around in his head. Knowing this was the opportunity to come clean himself. Ease her conscience by telling her about his own past.

Instead, he said, "You don't need to apologize, Elise. You don't owe me anything you aren't comfortable sharing. But for the record, if you want to talk about it, I'll listen."

Her lips pressed into a flat line as she nodded too quickly, blinking back tears.

"It's just hard for me to talk about. Hard to deal with. But at least if I'm the only one dealing with it, then when I don't want to think about it—when I want to pretend it's like it always was, I can. If you don't know what's happening, then you won't ask me what kind of day my dad is having. What the latest news is on his medication. If he's getting worse." She swallowed, and closed her eyes a second before snapping them back open and scanning the streets.

Levi slowed the car, giving her time to reassure herself she hadn't missed anything. Settling back into her seat, she went on. "Sometimes I just need to forget—be someone without all the worries."

Someone without all the worries.

He understood the need to be someone else for a while.

To take a break from the problems. But he also understood something else. "This is why you can't come with me. Why leaving town, even for a few months, isn't an option."

"And why the studio is so important. It's not just for me."

No, he'd imagined it wouldn't be. "What are you thinking?"

"That my mom's spent the last six years at home taking care of my dad. Giving up a little more of herself each year, because she wouldn't consider giving up the time she had left with him. Didn't want to risk speeding up the progression of the disease with a change in surroundings or by bringing in unfamiliar faces. She just kept telling us she could handle it. Refusing to even consider that Dad might be at a point where he needs more help than she can give him. But after this—something has to change. And she's going to need something to do. A place to go, to start rebuilding a life that doesn't revolve around someone who mostly doesn't know who she is anymore."

He got it. "And you're going to be ready. With a place for her to come."

"She needs to be around people again. Get out of that house for more than a trip to the doctor's office. The studio would be a base where she could spend some time with me. If she wanted to work, she could help out with the child care or handle the front retail area. I just want her to have options. I want to give her something she can count on."

Because Elise knew what it was to feel as if her options were gone. To suddenly have everything she'd counted on taken away. Levi's fists clenched over the wheel.

Yeah, now he got it, all right.

He hated that she had to go through this. But at least she wasn't alone now. He'd stay with her, searching, for as long as she needed him to.

Reaching over, he slipped his hand beneath the tumble of silky curls at Elise's neck. "We'll find him." He just hoped to hell it was the truth.

Twenty minutes later, the phone chimed to life, the screen illuminating behind the white-knuckled grasp of Elise's fingers.

Slowing at a deserted intersection, he waited as she quickly connected the call.

"What's going on?" she asked, still scanning the sidewalks. And then her head dropped forward, her free hand covering her face, and something wrenched deep inside his chest.

"Thank God. Where?… I can be there in—… Are you sure?… Okay, I'll see you then."

Disconnecting, she turned to him, eyes shimmering bright.

"He's okay?" he asked.

She nodded, her throat moving up and down in the exaggerated way it did with the buildup of too much emotion.

"Yes. David and Ally found him down by this restaurant we used to go to when we were kids. He's fine. Tired and worn-out—which may have been a good thing in getting him into the car…" Her voice trailed off, and she looked out the window into the darkness of night. "But he wasn't hurt."

"Do you want to meet them over at your parents' house? Is that where they're going?"

"It is, but they don't want me to come. David's going to stay the night and then in the morning I'll go over and we'll meet with his doctor. Talk about options." Leaning back into the seat, shoulders sagging with relief, she closed her eyes. "Could you just take me home?"

She looked fragile in the seat beside him. At that moment, all he wanted to do was pull her into his lap and hold her against his chest. Promise her all kinds of nonsense about how everything would be okay. Only it would be a lie, one that neither of them could buy into. Levi didn't have a wealth of information about Alzheimer's, but he knew well enough what it was like to live with a disease that couldn't be cured.

His mother's alcoholism. At times she was recovering, but the disease itself would never go away.

Shifting uneasily in his seat, he tried to push the thoughts of his mother away. Only the parallel was too easy to draw, especially as his mother was currently unaccounted for. In Levi's case, however, there wasn't anything remarkable about that. She dropped off the grid most every time one of her short-lived bouts of sobriety splashed to an end.

CHAPTER FOURTEEN

BACK at her apartment, Elise dug into her pocket for her keys. Still shaken by the events of the night and particularly the rushed call from her sister when she'd gotten their father back to the house, she dropped them on the floor, then nearly stumbled trying to pick them up before Levi stepped in to retrieve them for her. Without a word he opened the door and, palm low at her back, guided her inside.

Taking her hand in his, he studied her face—brushed his thumb beneath her eye. "You're exhausted. Let's go to bed, honey."

She peered up at him, and suddenly it was all more than she could bear. All the emotion she'd been fighting to control, all the doubts and fears and needs and wants. Everything burst free in a choked sob too great to contain.

Her hands flew to her face and she tried to turn away, tried to hide, but Levi's hands were on her shoulders, pulling her back into his arms. "It's okay, Elise. You can cry, sweetheart."

And she did. She wanted to stop, but the strength of those arms around her were too much to resist. Levi was solid and warm. Capable. And he didn't back down or back away beneath the barrage of her tears. Instead he gathered her closer—one hand cupping the back of her head while his other arm banded across her body. Soothing her with that gruff, low voice she hadn't known could be so tender. "Shh. I've got you."

Her forehead pressed against his chest, finding the center shallow that seemed made just for her. "He hasn't recognized me for months. Every time I see him, he's slipped further away. I barely recognize him as the man who raised me and—Levi, when they got home, my mom had a black eye. He'd gotten so agitated this afternoon—she said she couldn't calm him down and it was just an accident, but…"

Levi's hand stilled where it was, his whole body seeming to tense around her. And then his arms slipped tighter, holding her more securely than she could ever remember being held. "Has that happened before?"

She shook her head. "My dad? Never." Her throat constricted. "He wouldn't raise a hand to any of us. Which makes it all the worse. This disease has stolen him from us. From me. Taken the constant he's always been and turned it into something else."

"No. What your father's been to you isn't something that can be taken away. Your dad may not have the ability to remember it, but you will. He'll always be with you. A part of you. That relationship is the foundation of who you are. No matter how you build on it, that love is always going to be there. Even when he can't be anymore."

Fingers smoothing the fabric of his shirt, she whispered the only words she could manage. "Thank you."

Levi held her a minute longer, then ducked down to catch her behind her knees.

Cradled in his arms as he carried her back to her bedroom, she peered up at him. "You don't have to do this."

"You're light. I'm strong. It works," he offered, deliberately misunderstanding her.

"I'm a mess. You don't have to stay."

Levi's chest rose and fell on each breath. His heart hammering a steady rhythm beneath her ear.

"Yeah, I do." He hit the hall lights before turning into her room.

"I'd be okay."

"I wouldn't be." Levi sat on her bed, his back against the headboard, legs outstretched, arms holding her against him. "I'd worry, wondering if you'd been able to sleep. I'd spend the night thinking about how much better it would have been if I were holding you instead. For now, just let me take care of you."

Her throat tightened around a well of emotion she didn't want to try to name and she nodded against him. In that moment, she realized he was everything she'd been telling herself she wasn't ready to have. He was kindness and understanding. Humor and support. Tender strength and unfailing generosity. The kind of man who would be there for her—if he weren't leaving in less than a month's time.

CHAPTER FIFTEEN

As days of the week went, Sundays were a long-standing favorite with their slow pace and quiet vibe. Elise worked most of them, usually covering four classes split between two studios catering to the morning crowds, but by noon she was free and clear, and today she couldn't wait to get home.

When she'd left at six, Levi was still in bed—all naked, stubble rough, and sound asleep—and, more than anything, she'd wanted to crawl back under the sheet and close her eyes. Let the strong arms that had held her through the night close around her again, and give into the bliss of Levi in her bed. Only as tempting as that enormous masculine body was sprawled across the too small expanse of her bed, she knew better than to risk getting within arm's reach. A semiconscious Levi, intent on getting her body tucked back against his own, was not as receptive to reasoning about work commitments as she might need him to be.

On her first attempted break from her bed that morning he'd offered to write a note excusing her from class. When she'd mentioned a note wouldn't get her paid, he offered to cut her a check. For a thousand bucks.

Rounding the corner, her smile spread wide and her pace picked up as she remembered the sound of that low growl of satisfaction when he buried his nose in the curve of her neck. Somehow—even with the emotional turmoil of moving her father into a special care facility this week, the hours of paperwork, and nerves running rampant through her family—Levi had kept her sane. Reminded her that she could smile. Shown her she wasn't alone.

A flash of white caught her eye and Elise squinted down to the far end of the block. To Levi, walking her way with what looked like a paper and pastry bag in one arm and a drink tray with two coffees in the other. She wanted to blame the acceleration of her heart on her hastening steps to meet him, but it wasn't true. More and more, it was just Levi. Doing things to the center of her chest with his grin, the strength of his arms around her, that look he gave her when she caught him off guard. His candid talk about business strategy, that easy laugh, and the way he made her feel so intensely wanted by somehow finding a way to touch her nearly every minute they were together.

Levi pressed a quick kiss to her lips and held his bounty up for display. "Hey, beautiful."

The way he said that pushed her belly into another round of acrobatics. "You got food?"

Levi dug into the bag with a nod. "Doughnuts. From the place you like. Let's sit in the park."

Elise nodded, always fond of Printer's Row Park and the small fountain there.

Seated on a bench, he passed her a chocolate-glazed doughnut, napkin, and coffee, then asked about her classes. "Mrs Fitz there this morning?"

Coffee halfway to her mouth, Elise paused. She'd told him about the sixty-eight-year-old eccentric—with form and strength that put hers to shame—weeks ago. *And he remembered her name.*

"She was." And wearing one of the skimpiest yoga get-ups Elise had ever seen.

Absently sorting the sections of the paper, Levi grinned. "This is the class over at the athletic club, right?"

"Yeah, you should get a day pass just for a look at her. Or maybe not. Even closing in on seventy, she kind of blows me away."

Levi chuckled. Elbows resting on wide-slung knees, he flipped open the entertainment section of the *Trib*. "Not possible."

A warm breeze rustled the edges of the paper and teased through the strands of his dark hair. Elise leaned into the right side of Levi's broad back, felt the vibration of his gruff, "Nice," against her cheek where it rested on his shoulder.

Closing her eyes, she told herself to just take this moment. To hold on to it for the beautiful simplicity it offered and not to let the panicked emotions pushing at her throat free. Not to give in to those thoughts fast on the rise that were suddenly demanding to know what she was going to do when Levi left.

Because somehow, against all her best intentions, in spite of all her defenses, she'd gone and fallen in love with him.

She was over her head, and getting deeper every minute…even knowing that every day was one day closer to the one where he left town for good.

Suddenly it was all too much. The loan, the studio, her parents, her future, and the one thing that felt so totally right on the cusp of being over. Her head spun and her stomach seized. The open air around her turning thick and stale in her throat.

She jerked to her feet, stumbled back.

"Elise?" Levi was on his feet reaching for her as she desperately fumbled her keys.

Get inside. She had to—

Too late. Her stomach heaved and she lunged for the trash bin.

Inside, Levi wrung cool water into the sink and then pressed the washcloth to the back of Elise's neck where she sat on the side of the tub, head bowed.

"I'm fine, Levi. Completely better now, though I'm not sure I'll ever recover from the humiliation of you seeing me get sick. And in public."

"Glad you're recovered." Only not really. Staring down at Elise's slender back, the silky curls tied out of her face, and the delicate hands pressed against her eyes, Levi would have felt a hell of a lot better if Elise were still hugging the porcelain bowl, cursing a sketchy breakfast sandwich consumed some time in the last few hours. But no, the nausea that hit her out of nowhere was gone as quickly as it had come. And the only reason she was still sitting in here was because Levi hadn't let her up yet.

He needed a minute.

Not because he couldn't handle the sight of a woman vomit. Courtesy of his mother, he'd been hardened to that at an early age. So seeing Elise pitch at the park was about as close to old home week as he got. The only thing missing was the sinus-burning fumes of cheap liquor in the mix.

No, what had Levi's gut wringing harder than the cloth in his hands was the short list of reasons women were suddenly, violently sick to their stomachs. Without a fever.

Yeah, Levi had definitely needed a minute.

To do some math. To think back…very carefully…and come up with a whole lot of *holy hell*. He couldn't recall more than two nights at a stretch they hadn't seen each other. In over a month.

Catching sight of himself in the battered rectangle of

mirror above Elise's single bathroom sink, Levi tried to re-arrange his features into a mask of something that at least resembled calm. It wasn't working.

Tossing the washcloth into the sink, he stalked out of the bathroom before Elise could get a look at him.

"Levi?" Elise sounded tense behind him.

Because she wasn't sure how he'd take her blowing the contents of her stomach in front of him?

Or because she had something she hadn't been ready to tell him…and she'd just given him a very big clue.

Gripping the back of the couch in the front room, Levi stared at the window, seeing nothing beyond. Just feeling the slow press of the walls around him. An incremental tightening of his skin.

God, it couldn't be that.

"Levi, I don't know what to say. I'm really embar—"

He turned, staring hard at her. "Are you pregnant?"

"What?" Confusion flashed in those guileless gray eyes. Confusion followed close by horror. "You think be-cause I—" Her hands waved in a small churning circle. "No— Oh, my God, no." Her shock was genuine. No one could fake that level of stunned distress—or at least Elise couldn't.

"No. I can't be."

That was the answer he'd been hoping for. Only between that breath and the next, Elise's eyes lost their conviction and her face went pale.

Damn it.

"Let's just start simple. When was your last period?" This wasn't the kind of conversation he typically had with his dates. But then most of his dates barely registered as more than a blip on the radar. And no, it wasn't that he didn't think they could get pregnant because he only slept with them once or twice. It was more that the kind of women he generally went out with tended toward the more sexually practiced. So in addition to his religious condom use, there was typically another form of birth control in play. The pill. The patch. An IUD. Something.

But Elise. She didn't have the kind of lifestyle where she was looking to be prepared just in case something came up. Which meant the condoms he'd been packing were flying solo. And they weren't one-hundred-percent effective.

A small furrow dug between Elise's eyes as she pinched the bridge of her nose with one hand, using the other apparently to count on her fingers. The muscles along his spine cranked tighter.

"Aren't you supposed to know this kind of thing?" he bit out, the words coming more harshly than intended.

A rush of pink surged up Elise's neck and into her cheeks, making him feel like an ass of the worst variety. But this was important. For both of them.

"Okay, let me help you out here. Before you met me or after?" There were only two options; how could she not know? *"Elise."*

"Just give me a minute." Her voice had taken on a frantic edge to match the one cutting through his gut that very moment. "My cycle sometimes skips and honestly I don't always pay a lot of attention to it."

His vision tunneled. *"You don't pay attention to it?"*

"No, Levi. I don't. It's never been particularly reliable and, aside from the fact that I have just a few other things going on in my life, before you, I hadn't had sex in over a year. So no! I hadn't paid it much attention lately."

Unreliable.

His sanity clung to the concept like a lifeline as one breath filled his lungs, and then the next. His heart slammed, pushing blood in a rush too fast through a system already jacked on fear and dread.

"Before." She looked up at him with a little-girl-lost stare too vulnerable for the place he was at. "It was definitely before."

CHAPTER SIXTEEN

ELISE sat in the corner of the couch, her legs drawn up close to her body with her arms wrapped tight around them. Holding herself together. Or trying to, anyway.

It had been about six weeks since her last period. And though she'd told Levi it wasn't the first time she'd been that late, the information seemed to have pushed him past his limit nonetheless. She'd watched, helpless, as he walked from the apartment without a word, leaving her alone in a way she hadn't been since the day she met him.

Brows pressed against her knees, she breathed deep.

She couldn't be pregnant—couldn't believe she was. Wouldn't she have felt some change in her body? A connection to something bigger than she, and yet contained within her?

Granted, her life was full in a way she wasn't exactly accustomed to these days. The distractions vast, each one more consuming than the last. But she hadn't sensed… anything.

Even at Levi's prompting, all she felt growing within her was denial.

The certain sense that it simply couldn't be. It wouldn't be fair. After all the waiting. After all the work. To finally be so close to reaching her goals— A pang of guilt struck her hard in the chest.

Selfish.

If she was pregnant, there wouldn't be any room for that kind of thinking. Their baby would deserve better.

Their baby...

Hers and Levi's. This thing between them wasn't supposed to be anything more than a single night. It wasn't supposed to turn into something Elise had begun wondering if she could live without. It wasn't supposed to be love.

Levi was leaving in three weeks' time.

But a baby would change everything.

A baby was forever.

More important than the plans she had for her studio. More important than anything. And though the idea of her life changing so radically scared her near senseless, Elise realized one thing... She wouldn't be alone.

All the ways that Levi had surprised her over the last month came rushing to the fore. His generosity and confidence. The way he forced her to let him be there for her even when she'd tried to push him away. He was more than she'd expected. More than either of them had given him credit for...and if any of these fears were grounded and they were having a baby together...she had faith that together they'd make it work.

The front door opened and closed with a muffled thud, followed by the jangle of keys landing in the clutter catcher.

Elise was off the couch in a blink. It hadn't bothered her when he'd left the way he had. The threat of everything changing so drastically—all the plans they had would have to be reshuffled. She might have been more concerned if he'd taken the whole thing in stride. But hearing that front door close, she hadn't quite realized the way she'd been waiting for him to come back. How desperately she'd wanted to be with him. Have his arms around her and his common sense and straight thinking in her ear.

How much she'd needed his reassurance that everything was going to be okay.

She'd nearly closed the distance to him—the need within her pulling faster than her feet could move—when he stopped her by holding out a nondescript brown paper bag between them.

"Pregnancy tests."

Elise took the bag and tipped the contents into her hand. A two-pack of over-the-counter stick tests.

Of course. It made perfect sense. And Levi was always thinking.

The lines in his face were etched deep, fixed with strain. Reaching out, she smoothed a hand over his arm. "Are you okay?"

Stiffening beneath her touch, Levi took a cool step back. "I guess we'll find out in the next few minutes or so. Though the pharmacist said a negative result on one of these sticks doesn't guarantee you aren't pregnant."

She'd heard that before from Ally when she'd been trying to get pregnant and had to pee on six different sticks over two weeks before she'd finally gotten the positive result. There wasn't nearly the wiggle room if the reading was positive.

Stuffing his fists into the front pockets of his jeans, he nodded at the boxes. "Look, why don't you take the first test?"

"Sure," she answered, nerves once again turning her stomach against her.

She peered across the canyon opening between them. Levi looked hard and unyielding. Utterly unavailable to her.

Wrapping her arms around her middle, she tried to assure herself she was just being sensitive. Emotions were running high, and she was reading more than she should into what was probably a completely normal reaction.

Levi was as overwhelmed as she was. Once they got the results—once they knew where they stood—he'd be able to respond the way she'd come to expect him to.

Picking at the outer packaging, Elise headed down the hall to the bathroom, only realizing that he'd been following her when she muttered a curse at her inability to get past the cardboard and Levi reached over her shoulder and grabbed the box.

He planned to follow her into the bathroom.

They'd shared a lot of things over the past month, but this wasn't one of them.

Stopping him with a palm at the center of his chest, she shook her head. "Just give me some privacy and I'll be right out."

The lines between his brows dug deeper, the angles of his features going harder as if he were bracing to object. But then his eyes met with hers and he took a step back.

The two minutes Levi had been standing on the far side of that bathroom door felt like the longest of his life. But then the door swung open and Elise stepped tentatively out. Over her shoulder, he spied the slim white stick of plastic resting on the side of the bathtub, looking about as innocuous as a bomb about to detonate.

Elise raised her hand toward him, but then let it drop and stepped past. "It says to wait three minutes. We can set the timer on the microwave."

Holding up his left arm, he answered, "I set one on my watch."

"Well, then, I'd like to get a glass of water."

He didn't want to leave the doorway. Didn't want to let that little stick with its tiny window out of his sight. Hell, he hadn't even wanted to let Elise take the test without him there to ensure she did it correctly. Not because he didn't trust her to be honest with him, but because it was just too damn important.

Elise was staring at him expectantly. Waiting for him to follow her back to the kitchen, he assumed. Fair enough. Rationally, he knew his presence wouldn't impact the results or timing of the test. And yet forcing his feet to move proved nearly impossible.

With a nod, he followed her back to the small table and chairs. "Sit down, Elise. I'll get you some water."

The legs of her chair scraped over the floor behind him as he ran the tap a second before filling a glass. The kitchen was too small. Cramped. Outdated.

Turning back to Elise, he set the water in front of her. "You'll have enough money to move. Buy a little house or something. If that's what you'd like." Although a part of him thought a building with a doorman might be safer. Maybe something down in Streeterville, like in the 680 building on Lake Shore Drive. There was a market, coffee shop, salon, security, parking—

Gray eyes gone wide with confusion blinked back at him. "What?"

"This apartment is fine for you, but if you're pregnant, you'll probably want something bigger. Safer."

A nod.

Good. He didn't want to have to argue with her about it. Only as the seconds ticked past he almost wondered if arguing wouldn't have been a step above the silence.

He didn't like it.

They'd eaten at this table a dozen times. He'd laid Elise back and treated her body like dessert on it at least twice. It was always with the laughing and the talk with them. But not now.

A frown pulled at Elise's mouth as she traced the beads

of condensation on her glass. "What did you mean, I'd 'have enough money to move'?"

If the woman sitting across from him had been anyone other than Elise, he might have waited to get a lawyer involved before having this conversation. But with her, he just wanted to be straightforward—alleviate whatever concerns he could. She wasn't mercenary. His finances had never been a topic of discussion. Hell, she probably didn't have a clue what his worth was.

She'd been trying to build a life for herself and all her plans were about to change. She needed to know she'd have some security.

"I mean that I'll take care of you. Both."

Relief swirled in those soft gray eyes and Elise leaned forward, her hand moving to cover his. "You say it like it's a done deal. We don't even know if there is a 'both.'"

Elise squeezed his hand, but Levi was too numb to feel. Still, watching the way her fingers worked through his was a comfort. She'd be one of those mothers who couldn't stop touching her kid. The one with so many kisses, the little guy would have to beg her to stop before they got to school and she embarrassed him in front of his friends.

He'd seen those kids. Rolling their eyes and making their protests as they tried to stiff-arm their way out of the kind of hugs he'd never known.

Eyes drifting to her glass of water and the bananas on her counter, he knew she'd be a good mom. There would always be food in the house and—

"I could just be late. I'm probably just late."

"I'll give you the money for the studio up front." He had it, and the last thing she'd need was to worry. "You'll be able to hire another instructor to replace you. If you're up for it, maybe you can teach a class for expectant mothers, and then work the front with your mom or help out with the childcare you were talking about providing. It'll keep you involved and social. Help you build a network of other mothers."

"Levi, wait," she said with a small laugh that somehow eased the worst of what was eating him. "I know you like getting everything all fixed up, but you're getting ahead of yourself. Whatever happens, we'll figure it out together."

Together.

Levi looked at Elise across the table, watching him with a combination of trust and tenderness in her eyes. And suddenly he was angry. None of it belonged there.

He knew what she was thinking. Knew how far off base it was.

"Elise, you're never going to have to worry about money. But that's all I've got to give you."

The little smile on her lips faltered. "What are you talking about?"

"I'm not the kind of guy you'd want in your kid's life. I'm good at two things. One got us to where we are right now. The other is developing clubs I sell for a lot of money. I can give you financial security. Real financial security. And if your needs change, if you need more than what we've arranged, I'll only be a phone call away."

Elise stared at him blankly, then shook her head, pushing away from the table. Her voice sounded cool, forced, as though it was taking everything she had to keep from screaming. "I think I'm misunderstanding. It sounds like you're not planning on being around…at all."

"Believe me, Elise. It will be better for everyone if I'm not."

Elise just blinked, confusion swirling in her eyes until he saw the realization strike. The hurt settle in. And whatever hopes or expectations she'd been fostering about him fade away. "You're telling me, if I'm pregnant, you won't want anything to do with me or this baby?"

"That's *exactly* what I'm telling you."

CHAPTER SEVENTEEN

TENSION gripped him in a vise cranked so tight Levi half wondered if he was going to snap.

Elise's soft eyes had gone to slate. "What kind of man would say that?" she demanded.

"The kind who's honest enough to admit he wouldn't make a good parent." The kind who'd been telling her he wasn't the good guy she deserved from the start.

The bitter huff of humorless laughter that answered told him exactly what Elise thought of his answer. That it was bull. A cop-out.

Only it wasn't. He knew firsthand what it meant to be better off without someone. Or a string of someones. He knew what it meant to have your hopes crushed over and over. To be let down by the person you needed to count on most.

He wouldn't do that to his own child.

Reluctantly his mind dragged him back through the years to a rat-hole apartment, and the nightmare that was having nowhere to run, no way to hide. To the lead weight in his small gut as he crouched in the corner, wishing he hadn't come inside—but the cops had driven past the alley twice already and he was scared Child Services would get him. Scared of the stories his mother had told him about the kids who got picked up by them. So he'd come back and walked into another sloppy, booze-fuelled fight on the brink of violence.

The loser who'd been knocking them around the last two months was threatening to leave, his already ugly face twisted and red. Levi waited for the rest of the scene to play itself out—his mother's slurred insults and demands that the guy go.

Only this time, it was different. This time, she pleaded through her tears, clinging to his arm not to leave her. Swearing the baby had been an accident.

Promising she'd get rid of it.

At eight years old he hadn't fully understood what she'd meant, but it scared him anyway. He wanted to tell her to let the guy go. They'd be better off without him. She could keep the baby and he'd be good. He'd help her. He knew how to do lots of stuff on his own. He'd taken care of himself for that week she'd been gone the year before and he took care of his mom all the time. He even knew how to make money—only a little, but it was enough to buy food when he had to.

The guy called his mother pathetic and took a step toward the door, his foot landing on an empty bottle. He tripped, turning angrier than before. It happened fast. The backhand that sent his mother to the ground and Levi lunging across the room in flurry of fists and kicks that ultimately did nothing more than set the guy off worse than he already was.

The blow that came next was closed fist and the last he remembered.

He had to stay in for a week until the bruise healed, his skin itching from the inside out with the need to escape the dank space that reeked of stale smoke, booze and the guy who'd decided to stick around after all. For a while, anyway.

There wasn't any more talk about the baby or getting rid of it. And for a while Levi let himself hope, but by his next birthday his mother's body hadn't changed. No baby had come. And he knew it never would.

Eventually the guy left for good. Same as the others before and after.

But Levi couldn't. He'd just watch them leave, one after another, each year wishing more and more it could be him. Aching to get out, but knowing he couldn't go. Suffocating in the life he couldn't escape until finally it was his turn.

And once he left, there was no tying him down again.

He couldn't stand it.

Some people weren't cut out to have kids. People like his mother, whose dysfunction found its beginning and end in the bottom of a bottle. And people like him, who didn't know anything else.

It was just like he'd told Elise about her father. That relationship was a foundation on which the rest of her life had been built.

Levi's foundation was damaged to the point where no one was fool enough to build upon it.

He knew what he had to offer.

Money. Lots of it. Earned off a career based on leaving everything he'd built behind.

When it came to security though, the kind he'd never known, Elise would be the only one who could offer that. She'd be the kind of mother he'd wished he could have had.

He'd make sure nothing got in the way.

Elise wouldn't have to struggle. She wouldn't have to tie herself to some jerk-off just to get by. She knew how to love. She understood responsibility. And the cold look in her eyes when she realized he wasn't the kind of man her baby deserved told him everything he needed to know.

They would be fine.

And he would be too.

The trill of Levi's watch cut through Elise's bitter disbelief. Just three short minutes...how could everything have changed?

Together they pushed back from the table.

Vision tunneling, Elise walked on numb legs toward the results that would set the course for the rest of her life.

Levi followed close until they got to the bathroom, where he hung back at the door.

Reaching for the little white stick with trembling fingers, she closed her eyes and took a steadying breath.

Negative. It had to be.

She couldn't be pregnant. Not feeling as hollow as she did in that moment.

Blinking, she stared down as all her fears and hopes coalesced into the quiet sob that broke from her lips.

She waited for the relief to wash through her and drown out everything else. Only it didn't come to abate the sense of loss that had overwhelmed her before the timer had even sounded.

Feeling more tired than she could remember, she gave into the pull of gravity and sank onto the side of the tub, holding out the stick for Levi. She couldn't look at him. Not right then. Not with the cacophony of emotions clattering around inside her.

"What's this mean?" he asked, his voice hoarse.

"Negative. It's your get-out-of-jail-free card. Not pregnant."

Within the small confines of the room, she waited for him to say something. Let out a whoop of relief. Send up a prayer of gratitude. Something.

But the silence between them only stretched. She could feel his eyes on her. But couldn't sense whatever emotion was behind it.

Probably because there wasn't any. The guy was too cold for feelings. He'd been ready to write a check and walk away without a backward glance.

From his own child.

She shook her head. *No.* There was no child. She wasn't pregnant.

And yet she felt the betrayal as though she were.

Levi took the test from her hand. "They aren't a hundred percent accurate."

No, they weren't. "I'll take the other one in the morning. The hormones or whatever causes the reaction are supposed to be more concentrated then. I'll call and let you know."

Another pause, and she wondered if he was going to make her say the words.

Ask him to leave.

Why wouldn't he? He'd planned on asking her to raise his child on her own. What were a few uncomfortable words.

But then the floorboards creaked beneath the shift of his weight and he cleared his throat. "We'll talk tomorrow."

Elise wasn't pregnant.

Levi still couldn't quite get his mind around it. Couldn't feel the relief that should have been the flip side to the dread accompanying the belief she was. The truth was he didn't feel much of anything. Hadn't since he'd walked out her door the day before.

Maybe it was fatigue.

After giving up on the idea of sleep he'd gone for a run around 3:00 a.m. Given up on that around five and dragged himself home and into the shower. Did some work until noon, when Elise messaged that she'd managed to get an appointment with her physician, who'd confirmed the results—citing stress as the most likely culprit behind her missed period.

Now, Levi leaned back in his office chair, closing out one spreadsheet after another. Dragging the plans and provisions he'd been making for Elise and a baby that didn't exist across the well-ordered computer desktop and into the "Trash" bin.

It was nuts, but a part of him was disappointed he wasn't going to be giving Elise the money for her studio. He'd even toyed with the idea of offering it to her regardless—as an investment. Only he'd discarded the idea as quickly as it came to him. The last thing he needed to do was find another way to bind himself to Elise.

And considering the follow-up text to the news that she wasn't pregnant—*"Free this afternoon? We need to talk."*—he imagined Elise wouldn't be too fond of the idea either.

It shouldn't have hurt. After all, she knew she was doing the right thing. And for all practical purposes, the relationship was already over—having ended with the words, *"That's* exactly *what I'm telling you."*

But when Elise opened her front door, it felt as though the man walking through it was a stranger. The neat kiss pressed against her brow belonging to someone she'd never met. The subtle underlying connection that had been so much a part of every moment spent with Levi…gone.

She recognized the body, but the man she'd thought she'd known wasn't anywhere to be seen, and the stark realization that maybe he'd never been there at all was another shocking blow to her heart.

The sad confirmation that her desperate hopes Levi would show up and say all the right things—somehow convince her he'd realized he could never actually do what he'd suggested; better still, that she'd managed to completely misunderstand the blatantly clear words he'd spoken—were futile. Another bitter pill to swallow.

She hadn't wanted to believe it. Couldn't truly, after Levi had done so much for her. Shown such generosity and affection. But maybe it was only because those acts had been on his terms. Maybe he was one of those men who gave and gave when it suited them, but couldn't be relied upon if you really needed something and had to *ask*.

She didn't know. Would probably never understand. But hopefully at some point, she'd get over it.

Elise pushed the door closed as Levi walked into the living room and settled into the facing couch. Elbows resting on his widespread knees, fingers steepled beneath his chin, he watched as she sat across from him. "Get any sleep last night?"

"Not much," she answered honestly. "Just thinking mostly."

"Yeah, same here." His eyes were steady on hers, the lines of his face etched deep with strain. "A lot to process."

She nodded, hating the space between them. The stiffness of the exchange.

But maybe it was better this way. Having Levi wrapping her up in his arms while they talked as she didn't talk with anyone else wouldn't make what was coming next any easier. And it had to be done.

Elise drew a breath, mustering the strength to say the words that had been running through her head the past twenty-four hours. "This isn't going to work."

She didn't know what kind of response she'd been expecting or hoping for, but it hadn't been the quiet approval in Levi's eyes. The calm assurance she was doing the right thing.

"We knew it wouldn't from the start, Elise. Yesterday's shake-up just changed the time frame."

Yesterday's shake-up. Again she bristled at the callousness that seemed so out of line with the man she'd thought she knew. The man who'd made her wonder if maybe—

More than the time frame had changed.

"You're right." She heaved the breath sitting heavy on her chest. Straightened her shoulders and pushed a smile to her lips as she stood from the couch.

She'd expected there to be more to say. The conversation to take longer. Had felt the weight of all she'd had to convey straining inside her. But the truth was, there weren't that many words. There wasn't any confrontation or debate to be had. No explanations necessary. Just a simple close to something that had become more complicated than it was meant to be.

All that was left was goodbye. Goodbye and her gratitude. "I want to thank you for the help you've given me as far as the studio goes…and with my dad and family. You were there for me in ways I hadn't expected to need. And it made a difference to me. A big one."

Levi pushed to his feet and rubbed a palm across his mouth. Studied the space around his feet before bringing his focus back to her eyes. "You carry a big load on those little shoulders, Elise. Don't waste your time with guys like me who can't offer you anything more than some business experience and a car when you need a ride. You deserve the kind of guy who's going to share your burdens. A life."

The way he minimized what he'd done didn't sit right with her. But the corner of her mouth pulled up regardless as she let out a quiet laugh. "You telling me to find a nice guy?"

Something dark flickered behind his expression and then it was gone. Replaced by Levi's own half smile. "That's exactly what I'm telling you."

CHAPTER EIGHTEEN

Ink flowed from the ballpoint of her pen, looping blue-black across the signature line on the lease Sandy had signed only moments before. And then it was done.

Elise leaned back in her chair and let out the breath she hadn't realized she'd been holding. The anxiety that had been twisting through her belly for days easing into a nervous hum that was more anticipation than fear.

They were on their way.

Sandy turned in her seat, head cocked to the side. "You were right about this. The location is perfect. I know it is."

Elise smiled back at her. "We're giving ourselves every opportunity for success. We'll start renovations and promoting this week and before you know it we'll be ready for business."

They talked for a while with the landlord before Sandy had to run for her next class. Elise stepped out into the sunshine of the early afternoon, the keys to her future held tight in her grasp.

Walking past the storefronts that would neighbor her business, she noted the potted flowers by the doors. The creative window displays. The bustle of pedestrian activity. Young mothers decked out in trendy sport attire, their boutique purchases hooked on their titanium stroller handles. Her future clientele.

One step closer to her goal, she should have been elated. Instead, all she could think about was Levi. How she wished she could share this with him.

How she wished things had been different.

It had been a week since he'd walked out her door taking more of her heart than she'd ever meant to give. She'd been angry and confused. Overwhelmed and at loose ends, trying to understand how she could have been so wrong about who Levi was. Only as the hours and then days passed, his actions and words from the time they'd spent together began playing through her mind on a continuous loop. She realized it wasn't that the man she'd fallen for hadn't been real, but that she'd been unwilling to believe in the limitations he'd told her about from the start.

He was generous and thoughtful and supportive and sexy…and in addition to all the wonderful things he'd been to her, he was also the kind of man who could tell her he would walk away from his own child without a moment's hesitation. Because, for some reason, he believed it was the right thing to do.

And she hated it. Hated herself for wishing she'd never found out the truth, for wishing she could have had those last few weeks with him. For wondering if maybe, given time, he might have changed.

Her steps came to a halt on the sidewalk.

This was the day she'd been waiting for and she was celebrating alone, with a pity party in the middle of the street. Unacceptable.

She had news to share.

Within the cozy north-side bungalow, Ally sat at the edge of her pastel floral couch, eyes wide, hands up in the air. "Shut up! How could you not tell me?"

Elise laughed, delighting in her sister's over-the-top response to everything. "I didn't want to jinx it. But now with the loan through and the lease signed…"

"That is so cool! I'll tell everyone I know." She snapped once, pointing at the ceiling. "I'll post it on Facebook and get all my mommy friends to sign up. What did Mom say?"

"All the usual mom stuff about hard work paying off, how impressed she was, how proud Dad would be—he looked really good, by the way. Comfortable. And Mom seemed…relaxed. It was a great visit. Just what I needed today."

Ally's smile was understanding, a reminder of how truly lucky she was.

They talked about the plans for the studio and then invariably the conversation wound round to Levi. The advice he'd given her. Suggestions he'd made. And how Elise was managing since they'd ended the relationship.

Ally snugged down into a corner of the couch, stretching her legs out across the cushion. "So you really liked him."

Walking her fingers over Dexter's tiny chest, Elise nodded, her lips pinched between her teeth.

"He was there for you. I mean, clearly he was someone you could talk to about the studio. He came through with Bruno…basically daily. The night with Dad—that made all the difference. And there was that whole bone-melting thing."

"Yes."

"But when the chips were down, he walked."

This time even the single word seemed too much and she answered with a halfhearted shrug.

Ally pursed her lips and blew out a skyward breath. "Too bad. Pretty much anything short of that kind of responsibility shirk you might have let slide. And then you could have had the next couple weeks to let him make you melt."

The melting was definitely nice, but it was only part of what she was missing. And that was most of the problem. She'd gotten used to the companionship, discovered how good the kind of connection she and Levi shared could feel, letting herself get too deep with the wrong kind of guy. "Maybe Levi was right."

"Right about what?"

Dex's tiny fists worked frantically against his mouth as if he were trying to get the whole thing in. "I should find a nice guy."

Ally bolted upright, any signs of fatigue gone in a blink. "Like Hank!"

Grabbing Elise's arm, she searched her eyes. "I thought you didn't have time for a nice guy. You couldn't make him the kind of priority he deserved to be. I thought you weren't in the right place in your life. What about all that?"

"I didn't think I was. But this month with Levi…" She had to swallow back the emotions. He hadn't been in the way of the life she was building. He hadn't resented her for needing to plan their time together around two insane schedules. He'd respected her for it.

He'd supported her and made her feel as if what she was working for was not only worthwhile, but within reach if she kept her eye on the prize.

He'd been so different than Eric. Eric was a nice man, who'd wanted a nice life, with a nice wife and a nice family, but who wasn't so very nice about priorities that didn't align with his own. About commitments to people other than him.

Levi had shown her how different it could be. He'd given her a taste of what it was like to be supported. To know that if she fell, there would be someone to help her get up, dust her off, and encourage her to try again. He'd shown her that she didn't have to give up the parts of herself that were outside of her relationship, in order to have one.

Of course, Levi didn't actually want all the things Eric had wanted, and maybe that was part of the emotional disconnect that made it so easy for him to accommodate her. He wasn't worrying whether a few weeks' chaos would set the tone for the rest of their lives.

Whatever it was, briefly, Elise had felt as if she'd had it all.

God, she missed him.

"Hey, it's going to be okay, Elise." Ally's voice had gentled, the matchmaking gleam in her eyes fading to sympathetic understanding as she reached out and brushed something cool and wet from Elise's cheek. A tear.

Shaking her head, she let out a huff. "This is so stupid. I shouldn't be crying over Levi. *He was a one-night stand.*"

Ally cocked her head. "Come on, you've known he was more than that from about the word go."

"But he wasn't supposed to be. He wasn't supposed to be the kind of guy who could make me care."

"And he wasn't supposed to be able to let you down. I know."

Elise shook her head, looked at Dex.

Such a precious gift. Such a miracle.

She wasn't ready for a family yet. But some day she would be. And when that time came, she wanted to be with the kind of man who wouldn't walk away.

A man with priorities that matched her own. Which meant no more dating Mr. Wrongs.

Levi extended his legs as far as he was able within the confines of his first-class seat, returned a brief smile to the passing attendant who'd offered him everything short of a sponge bath through the course of the flight back from

Seattle. The trip had been a success. The architect and contractors were on track, Levi's development manager, Ron, was already lining up interviews for staff, and a buzz about SoundWave opening had already begun.

The wheels were in motion.

So where the hell was that heart-jacking rush of adrenaline that always accompanied the first deep push to the next project? He'd been waiting for it as a junkie waited for his next fix—counting on it to distract him from the relentless thoughts of the bendy little distraction he couldn't get out of his head.

Rivers and swaths of trees cut through the landscape of the far west Chicago suburbs beneath them. They'd be on the ground in less than five minutes. Pulling up to the gate and deplaning within ten. This was the last time he'd be flying into O'Hare for anything more than a connecting flight. At least as far as the next few years went.

If things had gone differently with Elise, maybe he would have come back a few times. Taken a Sunday to Tuesday and—

He needed to knock it off. Whatever they'd had was over.

Elise had seen the reality of who he was and what he had to give, and, like that, the fantasy ended.

Time to put it behind him. Well past time.

Of course, he'd been telling himself that for two weeks now.

Closing his eyes, he cranked his head around to one side, then far to the other.

"Neck tight?"

The flight attendant had her hand resting on the empty seatback beside him as she leaned into his row. She had a smile with a hint of wicked in it and eyes that flashed with a confidence that said she knew what she wanted.

No uncertainty. No vulnerability. No adorably awkward missteps.

She was familiar.

He'd never met her before, but he recognized the intent he'd seen in hundreds of interchangeable faces over the years.

"You look like you need to loosen up." One artfully sculpted brow arched in invitation. "What are you doing tonight? Maybe we could unwind together."

Predictable.

Nothing different about her. At least not that she'd decided to show him, and he sure as hell wasn't going looking for it.

Different had gotten him where he was now. Thinking too much about a woman too good for him. Feeling like there was a boulder parked on his chest and the space inside his body was missing a piece.

He didn't like it.

Different didn't feel good.

Levi angled toward the attendant, letting his gaze roam the bulleted highpoints of the woman in front of him.

Time to get *different* out of his head. "So, you like clubs?"

HeadRush was packed, the line to get in wrapping around two corners, the bars doing a stellar job of keeping up. The place was running without him, just as it should be. Which left Levi free to concentrate on flight attendant Holly and her ever-attentive band of coworkers. Only Levi had had enough of team fly-by-the-seat-of-their-pants.

He'd wanted to like them, really he had. Hell, they were based out of LA and flying out the next morning. You couldn't get much better than that when it came to unencumbering distractions. Except that they weren't actually distracting him at all.

He wasn't interested. Not in Holly. Not in Lana. Not in Holly and Lana, or any other combination on offer.

Not while thoughts of Elise were still whispering through his mind.

Going for his standard extraction, he leaned toward Holly's ear, careful to keep his face out of the stiff mass of hair that had seen its way from one end of the country to the other and back. "Excuse me, I've got to get this."

Normally, he'd activate the phone when he pulled it from his pocket, but conveniently enough the thing started its shimmy for attention before he'd even gone for it. Holding it up as example A, he edged out of the booth, promising to send a round on the house.

Glancing down at the legitimate message, Levi came to an abrupt halt. The air in his lungs going stale as the world around him pressed in, unrelenting, heavy and thick.

CHAPTER NINETEEN

ELISE blinked instantly awake—aware that she'd been pulled into consciousness by something beyond her own restlessness. A hard rain pelted the windows, but the insistent patter wasn't the culprit. Sitting up in bed, she glanced at the night side table and saw it was shortly after one. No message displayed on her phone and no other clues hinting at what had disrupted her sleep.

But it had been something...*a knock at her door?*

Adjusting her pajamas, she padded into the hall, the sound of her weight shifting the old boards beneath her feet. She cracked the front door to peer out, blinked her surprise, then quickly released the chain and stepped into the hall where Levi's heavy steps were taking him toward the stairwell.

Clutching her throat, she called after him in an urgent whisper. Caught her breath as he turned. "My God, Levi."

The man looked broken. Soaked through, as water dripped from the phone gripped tight in his hand. The pale blue of his shirt clung to his arms, chest, and shoulders. His hair fell in wild, sodden spikes, and his eyes looked so lost, she wondered how he'd found his way to her at all. "What happened?"

Levi opened his mouth, but nothing more than a choked cough escaped before his head sank forward with a series of slow negating shakes that had her by his side in a second. His arms opened to her briefly, but then fell away.

"I shouldn't have come." His voice rasped rough through the space between them, each word sounding as though the effort to form it had been monumental. "I just—I just needed to see you. It's late though, I—"

Elise stopped him with a quiet hush, stepping into his body, heedless of the cold and damp that instantly penetrated her thin pajamas. Strong arms closed around her, pulling her closer as a breath that felt like equal parts relief and misery teased through her hair. Banding her arms around his neck, she held fast. Offering the heat of her body and embrace.

It wasn't sexual.

It was comfort.

Contact.

Connection.

And something that, for whatever reason, Levi seemed desperately to need.

With her every shift, he gathered her closer, burying his face in her neck, gripping her as though nothing were enough.

"Levi, please," she whispered, her heart aching for him. "What is it?"

Another choked response. "I...can't. Just please...let me have another minute like this."

Working her hands free, she moved them to Levi's face. Holding him as she kissed his jaw, nose, and eyes, she whispered that she was there for him.

It didn't matter what had come between them before. Right now, tonight, whether he had the words to explain it or not, Levi needed her. And she needed to be there for him. To lend him some of the strength he'd given to her when she'd needed it most.

Her lips met his in a closed-mouth press of affection that lingered until her eyes fluttered open and caught in the deep blue pull of Levi's gaze. In the need that suddenly went beyond the bounds of this chaste embrace.

Without anything more than that steady stare between them, their lips parted, coming together an instant later in a press that was wholly different than the ones that had come before. Levi's hands fisted in the hair at the back of her neck, the gentle tug against her scalp a spark igniting her desire.

Urging her head back, Levi took more. The desperation of moments before transformed into something hot and demanding. Something as essential to Elise as it was to Levi.

More than contact, their kiss become consumption. Greedy and devouring. Deep and powerful—

Levi broke away with a gruff curse. Eyes haunted and hungry all at once, he looked down at her. "I didn't come for this. But, hell, Elise—"

"Come inside." Ragged breaths filled the silence as she pushed a few wet strands from his face. "Please."

Levi searched her eyes, then, satisfied with whatever he saw there, followed her in.

They'd made love.

There was no other way to describe the unhurried union that had been a connection on every level. Levi had taken her slowly, filling her body with his, so each deliberate thrust nudged her womb. Every stroke and return brushed the full length of her body. All the while, he maintained that soul-penetrating stare that made her feel naked and exposed and cherished and protected all at once. And then, for long minutes after, he'd pressed his brow into the curve of her neck, arms braced beneath her back so he could continue to hold her close, without crushing her.

She could have spent the night beneath the decadent weight of him, her fingers trailing slow circles around his back, but eventually he'd rolled off her and left the bed. A moment later she heard the shower running, and rose herself. The sky was still black, with no hint of predawn light, but she wouldn't sleep again.

After a quick change into a tank top and some thin sleeping capris, Elise fumbled through the cabinets, pulling out the coffee to start a pot while Levi showered. His clothes hung over the backs of the kitchen chairs to dry as she spooned grounds and filled the basin with water from the tap. When the first dark drops splashed against the glass she leaned against the counter thinking about the desolate look in his eyes when she'd found him in the hall. Something had happened that had upset him enough that the only consolation he could think to find had been to *see her*.

She'd never met a man who held himself more apart.

Building a life around leaving people and places behind.

But he'd told her from the start…with her it had been different. And once again, she couldn't help but wonder what would have happened if there had been more time for them. If maybe Levi would have let her become a person he didn't have to apologize for coming to when he needed someone. If he might have found something worth holding on to.

The shower turned off, and by then the small pot had brewed.

A steaming mug cradled between her palms, she followed the hall to her bedroom, stopping at the door.

Towel wrapped around his lean hips, Levi sat at the edge of her bed, elbows resting on his knees, a weary set to his hunched shoulders.

"Levi?" she asked, setting the mug on her dresser top.

"My mother," he said.

Bleak eyes met hers, drawing her into the room. To Levi's side where she pressed into the warm skin of his back, waiting for the words that would come next, confirming what she already knew.

"They found her three days ago."

His mother. A woman she'd known next to nothing about, beyond the fact that she was a piece of the puzzle that made Levi the man he was today. A man who, despite everything, she loved.

Tears pushed to her eyes as she whispered again and again how sorry she was, the words sounding hollow, too small for the kind of hole left by this kind of loss.

After a moment, Levi nodded. "Me too."

Taking his hand, she asked what happened.

"A maid found her in a motel room. Thought she was sleeping until she tried to wake her." Raking a hand through his hair, he coughed out a harsh breath. "I should have done something."

Elise stroked his back, offering the kind of logic Levi had always used with her. "You couldn't have known."

Levi shook his head, casting a chilling look over his shoulder at her. "I knew. She was drinking. I hadn't been able to get her on the phone, which is what happens when she starts up again. I called the guy who takes care of her groceries. The food he'd brought the week before was rotting on the counters. He cleared it out some, and stocked the fridge, but the place was a wreck. The next week he could tell she'd been there, but it was even worse."

Realization dawned. "She was an alcoholic."

A single nod.

"Levi, I'm so sorry. But you can't blame yourself for not being there." Especially considering the word *again,* a telling hint at a history of problems. Which made her wonder more about what Levi's life had been like growing up.

"Had she struggled with it for long?"

Old bitterness welled within him. Struggle seemed too strong a word…and yet he understood that was what it had been for her.

"My whole life. And probably most of hers, though I couldn't say with any degree of certainty." The truth was, in the sixteen years they'd shared a roof, the only things he'd really learned about her were how best to stay out of her way…when he needed to clean her up…and, most of all, not to invest too much in those brief periods of sobriety when she'd seemed to get her life in order.

Those had been the worst.

The hoping something had finally changed and maybe things would be different after all—only to come home from school one day to an empty apartment and an empty fifth lying on its side atop that old Formica table. Waiting out the hours or days until she showed up slamming into the apartment, glassy eyed, slurring. Apologizing to the new guy trailing her in, for the son she hadn't warned him about ahead of time. Promising the kid wouldn't be any trouble.

The lightest touch grazed his arm, anchoring him to the now, even as the lead weight of his past tried to pull him under.

"Is that why you left home when you were so young?"

"That's why." He could still feel the walls pressing in on him. The sense of slow asphyxia that accompanied a life he'd been helpless to escape. And then somehow, he was telling Elise all of it. The things he'd never shared with another soul. The pain. The fear. The clawing desperation to get out of there. Everything right up to the sting of the slap his mother landed across his cheek when he confronted her about the missing schoolbooks he'd been fool enough not to find a way to hide. The creeping numb through his consciousness as she threw the debt of his existence in his face, hissing her regret that she hadn't had the money to get rid of him when she had the chance.

How he'd heard it before. But that last night was different—because he'd just turned sixteen, and he could finally leave.

How he'd gathered all the cash he'd managed to squirrel away, gone to the store, and bought enough food for a week. Smoothed the remaining crumpled bills, and left the stack next to the cans of soup on the counter. He'd known it was a mistake to leave the money, that she'd just use it to buy more booze. But it was the only way he could walk out the door. And he *had* to go.

"I didn't think I'd survive if I didn't go." It was the right thing to do. He knew it now, as he'd known it then. "But I should have gone back for her. Once I'd built a life for myself, I should have done more to help her build one of her own."

Tears streamed down Elise's cheeks. Her eyes shining with both rage and sorrow.

He hadn't wanted her pity. He shouldn't have told her at all.

Voice trembling, Elise asked quietly, "What could you have done?"

Running a hand over the back of his neck, he let out a heavy sigh. "Something more than buying off my conscience with a few bucks for rent and groceries."

"You continued to send her money?"

Levi let out a humorless laugh. "Hell, no. She'd have drunk it and put herself on the streets. Then I wouldn't have been able to reassure myself she was safely stashed away on the opposite side of the country. I rented her a small house and hired a guy to shop for her."

Her lips parted as the connection formed. "Yes. Just like I was offering to do with you, if you'd been pregnant. It's what I do when I can't live up to my responsibilities."

A subtle shake of her head. "That's not what I was thinking at all."

"It should have been. It's the truth."

There was an unsettling freedom in the admission, the burden of a shameful secret being lifted—even if the guilt of the action itself remained. Maybe he'd just needed Elise to know.

Needed to give her one more reason to push *him* away. Show her another example—one that wasn't in the abstract—of what kind of guy he was, so she'd lose that unbearable look of compassion and affection in her eyes once and for all.

Hell, he was so messed up. He never should have come here.

But in an ironic juxtaposition, just as he hadn't been able to force himself to do the right thing with his mother, he couldn't do it with Elise either.

He couldn't stay away.

So he needed to *make her* stay away from him.

"Is it the truth? It sounds more to me like you've spent your life trying to take care of someone who never took care of you."

Levi opened his mouth ready to come back at her, only the arguments were beyond him. He was exhausted. Aching in a way he couldn't explain or understand. Fatigued of both mind and body. And Elise—who'd brought him into her home, her heart, her body—was beside him. Her arms looped over his shoulders. Soft cheek against his back.

She was holding him close, even as he all but begged her to tell him to go.

Elise emerged from the L station, dreading the walk back to her apartment, knowing that Levi was gone.

They'd spent the last hours of the early morning in bed. Levi's big frame fit snug against the smaller proportions of her own. Warm breath teasing through her hair.

When the alarm had sounded at five, she'd closed her eyes, and slid from the strong arms she wished would hold her for the rest of her nights, leaving Levi asleep in her bed.

Better to just go.

The night before hadn't been the beginning of something lasting between them. The only thing that had changed in those hours they'd spent together was her understanding of what made Levi the man he was. The way he was.

Her sluggish steps dragged slower and slower until inevitably she stood within the echoing silence of her empty apartment. Walking to the front window, she sank into the couch—giving in to the pull of gravity as she gave in to her tears.

CHAPTER TWENTY

THE sale of HeadRush was final. The keys turned over. Vendors notified. Paperwork complete. Levi had picked up the last of his dry cleaning, closed his account, and sold his car. All that remained of his disassembled life in Chicago was a bag with two days' worth of clothes and a laptop. The sum total of his personal possessions—three boxes, a bed, and his clothing—had already been shipped.

It had never bothered him before, but this time as he examined the barren apartment he stood in, noting its resemblance to the day he moved in and pretty much every day since, a sense of loss—of waste—washed over him. He'd lived in this space more than a year and he'd never made it his own. Never filled it with furniture. Never found anything he'd wanted to hang on the walls.

It was like a promise to himself, the every single morning assurance that he wouldn't be staying. He wasn't trapped. This place was just temporary and he could leave at any time.

Pathetic.

Thirty years old and he was still trying to get out of that dingy apartment with his mother, waiting for the chance to bolt. Refusing to hope for anything more, because he wouldn't risk the letdown when it didn't come.

He'd built his life around a past he'd never escape. Only

as he stood there, looking at the empty space that had surrounded him for as long as he could remember, he realized what he'd built wasn't actually a life at all.

He knew that now, because for the shortest time—he'd had one. Through those weeks with Elise his counters had been cluttered, his schedule insane. His heart full.

Different.

The kind of different that happened once in a lifetime. And losing it had been every bit as bad as he'd imagined it could be.

On the street, Levi flagged a cab. Slid into the back and gave the driver directions. Checking the airline tickets with a pat to his jacket breast pocket, he leaned against the worn seats.

One last stop to make.

Elise stared desperately into the blue eyes before her, nerves making her pulse skip. "I love you. But, I just don't know what you need."

Dex's quivery bottom lip jutted forward as his tiny face screwed up, turning a vivid shade of beet.

Oh, no. Here it came.

"No, no, no," she hushed, feeling a moment of panic. "It's not that bad, baby. Auntie will figure it out. Just—"

The wail pierced the air, nearly taking out Elise's left eardrum with it. Pulling him against her chest, she began the gentle, bouncy walk that always seemed to settle her nephew when Ally or David did it.

The baleful cries only intensified.

He'd had a good bottle. A small burp. A fresh diaper. She'd had him on his front. His back. Up. Down. Her pinky in his mouth, her hair in his fist—but nothing seemed to soothe the little man and a guilty rush assaulted her at the idea he might have been picking up her tension.

Levi was leaving today and it made her heart hurt to think of him being gone. *To know* she wouldn't run into him over at the lakefront or cross his path on the street. To know that he'd done what he always did and moved on.

Another city. Another club.

Another woman.

God help her, she couldn't stomach the thought. Didn't know what she'd do when she finally broke down and looked up the new club. Found the publicity shots of Levi wearing a few supermodels on each arm.

She had to stop. Distract herself and put Levi out of her mind altogether.

Only everything came back to him…and the same thought she couldn't let go.

He'd wanted more.

Dex let out another wail, his tiny mouth rooting around her collarbone between heart-rending sobs.

"Shh, sweetie. Auntie's got you." She rubbed his small back in a slow circular motion. Felt his fragile body stiffen and then, a second later, a juicy gurgle had her pulling her chin back to look down—as a hot splash of partially digested milk went projectile across her throat and chest, pooling where she held Dex's body against her own.

Her breath froze in her chest as the reality of what had just happened sank in with the sour liquid. Peering down at Dex, she saw he'd gone slack with relief.

So that's what was bothering him. Now she got it.

Which meant time to swing into gear. Get them both cleaned up before the belly full of mid-digestion spit-up soaking through into her pants made it to the floor or anything else.

At that thought, Dex flailed his little arm, sending scattered drops of fetid formula in an arc across the hall.

Elise started for the bathroom, desperately trying to

ignore the rancid cling of her clothes or the way the hot contents of Dex's belly had already gone cold against her skin. All that mattered was getting them clean and getting the mess contained.

Only halfway down the hall, she heard the knocking at the front door.

Risking a shallow breath, she muttered, "Oh, sure, Mommy's back *now*."

Reaching behind, she cranked the knob, letting it swing open behind her.

"You missed all the action," she called back over her shoulder. "Just come in and kick the door closed behind you. I need help in here."

Dex's little fingers splayed and slapped against her clammy chest, a curious expression on his face as Elise hustled into the bathroom and started the shower. At the creak of floorboards behind her, she said. "I'm thinking I just get in with him like this. Rinse and strip him while we're in there, and then hand him off to you while I finish."

She'd at least get the bulk of the spit-up rinsed out of their clothes and could leave them in the stall until she got a plastic bag or something to transport them over to the laundry—

"Okay."

Elise froze with her hand under the tepid spray as the low-spoken word reverberated through the small tiled room—setting off an avalanche of emotions through her heart.

Not Ally's voice.

Not even close.

Dex still clutched against her, she turned to the bathroom door—where Levi stood, dressed sharp in a pair of dark jeans and a midnight linen blazer over a white T-shirt, and looking as impossibly gorgeous and unavailable as ever with that black leather duffel hanging from his hand.

"I thought you'd be gone already," she whispered, her voice breaking over the words.

"I'm on my way out." Levi set his bag down and stepped into the small room, eyeing Dex warily. "This your nephew?"

She nodded, peering down at his little form wriggling against her and wondered what Levi would think of him. "I'm babysitting."

Levi's nostrils flared and he gave a short shake of his head. "Looks like fun. That water ready?"

It took Elise a minute to realize he was talking about the shower running behind her. And then another after that to figure out he was waiting for her to get in it.

That couldn't be a good idea. When she'd made the suggestion, she'd figured it was Ally she'd be getting the assist from. "You don't have to help, Levi."

His brow drew down, darkening the blue of his eyes. "But it would be easier if I did."

She didn't want to admit it, but, standing there with Dex starting to squirm in her arms, she knew it would be. "Yes."

Levi stripped off his jacket and hung it on the hook at the bathroom door. "Then get in before I pass out from the fumes coming off that kid and I'm no good to you at all."

Elise chuckled lightly. Really, what else could she do?

Levi kept a hand at her elbow as she stepped gingerly into the tub, seeming reluctant to move away even once she was in and the water was hitting her back. He adjusted the stream at the showerhead, and then stood with her, one hand at the ready in case she lost her grip on Dex.

"Your jeans are getting soaked. I'm telling you, I've got him."

"But once you start peeling him out of those clothes, isn't he going to be all slippery?"

A single look at Levi's face and she realized there wouldn't be any talking him out of the assist.

As it turned out, the second set of hands made all the difference. And fortunately for all of them, Dex was the kind of baby who loved water. He cooed and flailed his arms beneath the soft spray, even giving up a giant toothless grin when Levi squirted the tearless baby-wash over his belly.

And then he was clean, too clean to stay in her arms as she was still wearing the contents of his stomach.

Levi's brows furrowed in concentration as he took Dexter's small weight in his arms, holding him close to his body as he carefully lowered himself to the floor and leaned back against the sink cabinet.

Standing beneath the tepid spray, she couldn't take her eyes off the scene before her.

Levi was so careful. So gentle. Such a big man, cradling that little terry-wrapped body against his chest. His hands moving every couple seconds or so to readjust his hold, making sure he was supporting Dexter's head just right.

"That's perfect, the way you have him," she said, pushing a wet tendril back from her face. "He'll let you know if he wants to move."

"I think he's good. His eyes are closing."

The sound of quiet triumph in Levi's voice had her smiling—until he looked up at her, his gaze darkening as it ran the length of her body and back again.

Suddenly she was all too aware of the way her clothes clung to her like a second skin, their pull and weight, and the fact that she was going to have to take them off before she could get out of the shower and take Dexter back from Levi.

"I'm just going to finish in here," she said lamely, wishing she'd opted for some cute patterned shower curtain instead of the plain clear one that allowed more light into the shower. And Levi's unobstructed view.

Maybe he would be cool about it. Keep his eyes averted and his mouth shut.

"Take your time. I'll be right here," came the cocky response that was pure Levi and too much of a challenge for her to ignore.

"Big of you, Levi. Especially considering that little bundle of boy you've got there isn't wearing a diaper beneath his towel."

Five minutes later, Elise had broken the land-speed record and was scrubbed, fully dressed, and gently extracting her sleeping nephew from the cradle of Levi's arm and chest.

She didn't want to think about how well they'd fit together, or the tenderness she'd seen in Levi's every touch and movement. She didn't want to think about how well he could fit into the kind of life he didn't want for himself.

She wanted to get Dexter into a diaper and then down for the rest of his nap. Then she wanted to get through the last minutes with Levi before her sister returned. And after that, she wanted a few minutes to herself to cry. Because there wasn't a doubt in her mind that was how this was going to end.

CHAPTER TWENTY-ONE

LEVI followed a few paces behind as Elise carried Dexter into the living room and then knelt down beside the mat laid out as some sort of diaper changing pit stop. The little guy was out for the count, sleeping hard in a way that Levi envied.

He hadn't slept right since Elise stopped sharing his bed.

Diapering like a pro, Elise wrapped Dexter up like a football-sized burrito before putting him down in the pen set up in her bedroom. She moved with confidence—as if taking care of an infant was the most natural thing in the world to her. Just as he'd known she would if—

"So today's the big day?" she asked in a hushed voice as she took his hand and led him out to the hall.

Levi wasn't much of a hand holder. It had always been too intimate for the kinds of relationships he had. But with Elise, he just couldn't resist the temptation of taking more than he should. Even now, as she tried to step back, he didn't relinquish his hold—instead shifting his grasp to thread their fingers together.

It was selfish, no *probably* about it. But he wanted the connection through these last minutes.

"Not so big, but today's the day."

She offered a nod and a smile that didn't reach her eyes. The ache he couldn't get out of his chest intensified until there was nothing to do but pull her into his arms and hope the proximity made it better. Only it wasn't enough. He didn't feel better and the quiet sobs that racked Elise's shoulders told him it wasn't helping her either. And yet he couldn't make himself let go.

Couldn't do anything but hold her against him and press his mouth to the top of her head.

"This is so silly, I know," came her muffled words from against his chest. "You'd think with almost two months to get used to the idea that you were leaving, I'd have done better than this."

His hand cupped the back of her head, fingers sifting through the soft curls he liked best when they were spilling over his pillow, caught in the early morning sun. How could he tell her how much it meant to him that saying goodbye was so difficult? The last thing he'd wanted to do was make her cry, but as her shoulders trembled in his arms each tear was like a gift.

He'd spent so many years holding himself back from the possibility of any kind of emotional entanglement, he'd forgotten what it meant to be cared about by someone.

Though that wasn't entirely true.

You couldn't forget something you'd never actually had. And this, what he felt with Elise, was like nothing he'd ever known. Seeing her cry for him—it was heartbreak and heaven all at once. A selfish kind of torment, and his reveling in it only added merit to his assertion that he wasn't the kind of man she deserved.

Was this why he'd needed to come over here? To see if she'd actually cried over his leaving? What was wrong with him that he could need something so hurtful from another person.

From someone he cared about.

Levi ran his hand beneath the fall of her hair to catch her

jaw in his palm. Gently, he tipped her head back to meet her gaze. Only when her face was exposed to him, and he saw the shimmering wells of hurt overflow her eyes, trailing heartbreak down her satin cheeks—there was no relief to be had. No satisfaction.

Just the sharp, sudden awareness that his chest had been ripped open.

Another salty tear spilled free, cutting a fresh path of pain through the next layer of his heart, exposing a part of him he'd never let free.

Brushing at the wet streaks, he muttered a vicious curse. "I don't deserve your tears. I'm not worth even one of these."

She shook her head as if she couldn't believe what he'd said. "I think maybe you're worth a few."

Levi took her hands in his, held them against his chest. "I came here to say goodbye to you, but I don't know how."

"Kiss me," she whispered, her words feathering warm and soft over his knuckles.

Lowering his head, Levi closed the distance between them and pressed his mouth to hers. Over the past two months, he'd had the soft give of her lips beneath his too many times to count. He'd tasted and taken her with his tongue. Crushed and caressed her when he'd finally gotten her alone. Brushed against her with whisper kisses meant to drive her wild and make her beg for more. But this was the last, and it was too brutal to bear.

Levi broke away at the feel of Elise's fists balling in his T-shirt. It wasn't passion curling her fingers against him, but pain.

Pain he felt as if it were his own. Pain he wanted to take away.

Eyes the color of a sullen sky peered up at him. "Tell me

you won't be back. That you won't call. That if you come through Chicago again, you won't look me up."

Levi felt the twist of his gut. This wasn't how it was supposed to be. Everything felt so wrong, like maybe this time—

"Because if there's any chance I'll see you again, I won't be able to put you behind me. I'll wait."

Levi drew a slow breath, then asked the question he hoped like hell he didn't know the answer to. The one that scared the life out of him. "Why would you wait for me?"

Helplessly, she shrugged. The look in her eyes was the most devastating he'd ever seen. "Because I love you."

Running his thumb across the swell of her bottom lip, he shook his head. She'd gone and fallen in love with him. "Why would a smart girl like you go and do something like that? Haven't I taught you anything?"

Elise nodded. "Yes. You have."

She might have said more, but three rapid knocks sounded at the front door, and instead she smiled that crooked, tough little smile of hers and said, "Tell me good-bye."

He knew he should.

Only when he opened his mouth it wasn't what came out. "Say it again."

Her eyes welled anew as if the knowledge that her words meant something to him hurt her all the more.

Blinking back her tears, she repeated, "I love you."

That organ in his chest that had been suffering a slow dissection turned over, starting to beat anew, and suddenly he couldn't keep his hands in one place. Couldn't stop himself from taking her shoulders in his grasp, from running his palms over her back, from cradling her cheeks and brushing her lips, and threading his fingers through the sodden mass of curls and closing his hands to fists as he held to her.

"Then come with me," he urged, possibilities suddenly spinning through his mind faster than he could keep track of them.

He couldn't let her go.

Whatever semblance of acceptance she'd been managing crumbled under the blow of Levi's words.

"What?" she choked, her heart ripping to shreds as those deep blue eyes searched her face.

"We can make it work. I'll buy out the studio. We can—"

"No." She cut him off, her voice echoing the conviction. "We can't. I can't leave. I can't leave my family." Not when her father had just been moved, her mother was trying to find her way through this new stage in her life, and she'd finally brought all her plans to fruition.

And he wouldn't stay. *Levi would never stay with her.*

The seconds ticked past as he stared at her, that wild connection she'd never been able to resist flowing hot between them.

Another knock at the door. This one louder than the first and accompanied by Ally's muffled voice. *"Elise..."*

"Elise," Levi said, his voice gone gravel rough with intensity. But there wasn't anything left to say.

"You need to go."

She moved to pull out of Levi's grasp, felt that instant of indecision when he wasn't sure he'd let her. The sorrow-tinged relief when he finally did.

Turning toward the door, she forced enough strength into her words to ensure Ally would hear. "Hold on. I'm coming."

She needed to be strong.

Just a few more minutes.

Once he was gone, it would get better. Her body would

stop screaming to go with him when her mind knew she could never be happy if she did.

Her bare feet padded over the hardwood she'd trodden a thousand times before, each step feeling foreign, uncomfortably numb. At the door, she reached for the knob—only to have Levi grasp her arm and tug her full against him. Taking advantage of her gasp of surprise, he took her mouth in a kiss so devastatingly possessive, so intense, she couldn't begin to muster a defense against the claim of it.

Knock, knock, knock! "*Elise!*"

Breaking the kiss, Levi looked her square in the eye. "This isn't over. And I *will* be back."

Then hoisting his bag from the floor, he pulled open the front door. Elise barely registered Ally's squeak of surprise, or the way Levi dropped a quick kiss on her sister's cheek as he brushed past her and ducked into the stairwell.

Ally was in her face, fingers snapping in rapid repetition before Elise's eyes. "What the heck was that? And... oh, God...Elise, look at you. Are you okay?"

Okay? Aside from the fact that the man who'd just left had taken her heart with him? No. Not even close.

CHAPTER TWENTY-TWO

LEVI had been driving the streets for hours, moving through one neighborhood after another, keeping a mental tally of what was there and, more importantly, what was not. Every new start he made, this eyeing for opportunity was a critical part of the process. One he began immediately and then would spend another few days on, taking notes, asking questions. Making plans.

It got him grounded.

Got his head working in the right direction.

But block after block, the tension in his gut grew. The doubts whispering through his mind multiplied, until at last the streetlights flickered to life and a glance at the illuminated clock on the dash confirmed he'd waited long enough.

Levi's fingers tightened over the wheel as he signaled a lane change and then headed back the way he'd come.

Reaching his destination, he pulled into an open spot and stared across at the building, already under renovation. The front door swung open wide and a couple of guys covered in the grit and dust of construction walked out, apparently through for the night.

Not so for him.

Levi took a bracing breath, and then headed for the building.

Inside, the air smelled of sawdust, drop cloths covered the floor, and a couple of sawhorses balancing a sheet of plywood comprised the only furniture. Voices echoed from deeper into the space, and Levi followed the sound, stopping at the framed-in doorway when he saw Elise—yoga bag still slung over one shoulder, attention fixed on the carpenter giving her a rundown on the day's progress.

This was what he'd needed.

Part of it anyway. The rest he'd start working on when the guy with the clipboard took off.

Her focus was slipping.

From the minute Levi had left that morning, Elise had been forcing herself to function.

Sure, there might have been some going through the motions involved. Her afternoon classes certainly hadn't been the best she'd ever offered. Not great considering her reputation as an instructor was in no small way going to impact the success of the studio. But with her chest feeling as though someone had taken everything vital from within it, she'd done the best she could.

Now, listening to Ed talking about getting the electrician in and when the flooring would be delivered, the thoughts about Levi suddenly couldn't be ignored. God, she could almost feel him…smell him… Her eyes closed as a fresh wave of sadness washed over her.

The last thing she needed was to cry in front of Ed.

Under the guise of stretching sore muscles, she ran her hand over the back of her neck, using her cocked elbow to shield her eyes from view as she tried to get the blinding tears under control.

She'd blame it on the sawdust or something.

An allergy.

Possible if she'd been able to limit the emotional breakdown to a single renegade tear or two. Only once the waterworks started, the rest of her body wanted in on the action. She'd barely been keeping it together since Levi walked out the door—dismissing Ally with a lot of brave talk and philosophical rubbish about life and love, until she'd finally driven mother and son from the apartment... but it seemed the levee had burst, and now she couldn't contain the overflow.

Her shoulders shook as, mortified, she wrestled against the sob working its way out of her body.

And then strong arms were surrounding her, a gruff hush sounding above her head.

"Oh, Ed, no. I'm fine," she choked, desperate to get a grip—and to work herself out of the hold her contractor had on her. A hold that only confirmed how desperately she missed Levi—because in that moment she would have sworn the medium-build contractor had grown six inches and firmed up in a way that felt all too familiar. Felt like the arms she needed—

"Elise," came the low rasp of a voice she'd never mistake. "Aww, baby, you're killing me."

Blinking wildly, she cleared her eyes enough to look up. Up. Up, into the face she'd been aching for. Her breath leaked out with a fresh batch of tears and her fingers clutched into his shirt. The same soft white cotton T-shirt he'd had on that morning. The same dark jeans.

The same fathomless blue eyes, daring her with the depths she'd never explored.

"What are you doing here?"

Levi swept the pad of his thumb beneath her eye and then nodded to Ed behind her. "I'm sorry, but would you mind giving us a minute?"

Scorching heat erupted into her cheeks as she turned

back to Ed, who was graciously jotting a few notes as he stood over by the wall.

Without actually looking at them, he capped the pen and tucked the clipboard beneath his arm, starting for the door. "I'm about through anyway. Any questions, we'll sort out tomorrow."

"Thank you," Elise managed weakly, wiping a fresh tear with the back of her wrist.

One last nod, and then he was gone. Leaving her alone in what would be her studio, with Levi. Who wasn't supposed to be in this time zone.

Levi slipped the strap of her yoga bag free from her shoulder and hooked it over his own.

"I had classes this afternoon," she offered dumbly, suddenly at a loss for what to say. Or maybe too afraid to ask the question she wasn't sure she could handle the answer to.

"I know. Been waiting for you to get through them." His hand drifted down her arm so his fingers could thread through hers. "I would have picked you up, but I didn't know your schedule this week."

"You didn't leave." She really was a master of the obvious.

Levi cocked one of those devastating smiles at her. "I couldn't."

Her heart did a little flip as hope trod a new path through her veins. "Why not?"

There was a conspiratorial glint to Levi's eyes as he leaned into her space, dropping his voice to answer. "I left my jacket with my ticket in it hanging on the back of your bathroom door."

Elise blinked, her lips parting, though she didn't have the breath to pass through them.

He'd missed his flight. Which meant this goodbye that had been torturing her slowly for the past two months had been given another reprieve. Another twelve hours, maybe. Another chance to break down the last reserve of strength she'd mustered.

Another night in Levi's arms.

"When I got to the airport—"

"Let's get out of here," she urged, cutting him off.

It didn't matter how badly she was going to hurt tomorrow. If they had tonight—if they had the next seven minutes—she'd take them.

She had the rest of her life to get over this man. And deep down, that was exactly how long she imagined it would take. Which meant making the most of *right now*.

A burst of something that felt a lot like adrenaline shot through her system, pushing her heart to pound and her skin to heat. There wasn't any time to waste.

Stepping into Levi's body, she wanted to linger over the heat and strength he radiated, but instead she pushed to her toes and reached up to catch the back of his head with her fingers.

"Elise."

"Or we could stay," she whispered, thinking of the new wall in the back hallway. It probably wouldn't hold their weight, but it would offer privacy from the street. And Levi was more than strong enough to hold her up.

Her body surged to life at the memory of his hands on her thighs, her body moving at his direction. The thrust of his tongue between her lips and the hunger in his eyes as he filled her—only then it wasn't the hunger or heat in his eyes she was thinking about. But the soul-shattering tenderness that had filled his stare that last time they'd made love. The way he'd looked at her after. As if on some level, he'd wanted to love her.

Throat constricting, she tried to shake off the emotions. Tried to focus on the physical. On the feel good. On the back-against-the-steering-wheel out-of-control chemistry that could almost make her forget about everything else.

Hands riding the frame of her hips, Levi searched her eyes—without making a move to close the distance between them. What was he waiting for?

Her heart began a frantic pace. She didn't want any more tears. Didn't want any more heartbreak. Fingers curling into the short silk at the base of his skull, she just wanted—

"Elise."

She shook her head.

"No more talk, Levi." They'd already said everything there was to say. "We don't have time."

His gaze lowered, his brows drawing down, hooding his eyes in shadow. "We have as much time as you'll give me."

Elise ceased her attempts to bring them into closer contact and, bracing her palms over the powerful chest before her, pushed—craning back, needing to see as much of Levi as she could take in. Searching his face and body for the visual clues to decipher the words she didn't understand.

He meant tonight. As much time as she'd give him *tonight*.

It was what she wanted. What she'd been trying to accomplish pulling at him with everything she had... But sudden unreasonable bitterness rose at the carelessness of his words.

Didn't he understand how desperately she would grasp at even the thinnest evidence he'd meant more?

"What if I want forever?" She threw the words back at him, more broken plea than the confrontational challenge she'd intended them to be.

"Forever?"

Levi's face blanked and renewed dread hollowed her stomach, until slowly that stunned expression began to lift with the left corner of his mouth. And her heart began to thump in a way that resonated throughout her entire body, the surge of emotion and need threatening to override any reason-based organ.

All her goals and ambitions surrounded her—finally within her grasp. The tight-knit fabric of her family stretched across this city. They were there for her, as she was for them. Priorities she'd built her life around.

But with Levi standing before her, that little-boy smile on his man's face rooted in the words *forever*...she couldn't let him go. She couldn't give him up. Not without ripping the heart from her chest.

"You said we could make it work. That we could find a way." Swallowing past the nerves and emotions, she licked her lips... "I want to go with you."

CHAPTER TWENTY-THREE

LEVI didn't get tongue-tied. He wasn't the kind of guy to find himself at a loss for words.

He was a man who always knew what he was after, had a plan to get it, and the smooth rap to make sure it ended up his. Of course, the usual rules didn't apply when it came to Elise, as evidenced by the fact that she'd left him stunned, shaking his head in disbelief as he pieced through the six words she'd spoken, puzzling over how he must have misheard them.

Only as he looked into her face, saw the cascade of emotions rushing over it—fear, hope, love, and faith—he realized he'd heard her correctly.

Sliding his fingers into silky coils of her hair, he tipped her face to his and kissed her, slow and soft, before pulling away to meet her eyes.

"I can't ask you to give up the life you've built here. I wouldn't want to."

"But—" she started, her voice little more than a broken whisper.

"Don't." He stopped her with his thumb across her soft lips, and then his mouth. "Let me finish, sweetheart. I couldn't ask you to give up everything you love here, everything you've been working for—"

Stubborn girl wouldn't be silenced. *"I love you."*

Damn, he'd never get tired of hearing that. And he believed it. Felt it in the way she clung to him, saw it in the glittering emotion pooling in her eyes. Tasted it in the desperation of her kiss.

It was so much more than he'd ever imagined it would be. More than he'd believed he could have. More than he'd thought he'd feel.

His palm cupped the smooth skin of her cheek.

But it was there—love—wrecking his chest and tightening his throat, so the words that finally escaped it were heart-and-soul rough with their depth of feeling. "I love you too."

This time it was Elise who'd been struck dumb. Levi savored the moment, his mouth hitching as she stood wearing that baffled expression on her beautiful face.

Not one to waste a perfectly good opportunity to press his point, he gripped her shoulders and pulled her flush against him, took her mouth in a firm kiss and then held her away, enjoying the unrelenting tug of the smile at his lips.

Yeah, that felt good.

"I don't want you to have to give up anything you love. I know how important it is to make your dreams a reality. The satisfaction of achieving your goals. I don't want you to have to sacrifice your commitment to your family, so you can commit to me.

"When I look into your eyes like this—when I see what I'm feeling shining back at me in them—I want you to have everything."

More than that, he wanted to give it to her.

"But what about Seattle? SoundWave? What about your dreams and goals? What you want?"

"You still don't get it, do you?" He caught a soft spiral between his fingers, giving it a gentle tug. "I'm not a nice guy. I'm not selfless. So you better believe, I am going after exactly what I want."

At the flicker of those smoke-soft gray eyes, Levi let out a gruff laugh, catching Elise's face gently between his hands. "And before those nerves of yours conjure up some wildly unflattering and totally outlandish scenario about what I mean, let me make it perfectly clear. I'm talking about you. *You* are what I want.

"The clubs are a job, and I'm done making them my whole life. My development team has brought SoundWave this far, they're good enough to take it the rest. Yeah, I'll have to make a few short trips out, but I want to make Chicago my base." Levi swallowed hard. "My home. As for my dreams and goals—the only goal that matters to me is learning how to become the kind of man who's good enough that some day these dreams I can't get out of my head become a reality."

Turning her head, she nuzzled into his palm. Kissed the hollow there. "Tell me about your dreams."

"They feature this gorgeous yogilates instructor. Sometimes they're about all things her bendy little body can do. But mostly, they're about the smile on her face. The sound of her laughter." Levi bowed his head, pressing his brow to hers. "I dream about the kinds of things I can't ask you for now. The kinds of things that come with forever. I want them. I never thought I would, but, Elise, I want them and I'll do anything to make you want them with me."

Elise pinched her lips together. Swallowed once. Then twice more in an effort to regain some semblance of the composure she'd lost even before Levi's admission. How could he not see? How could a man so wildly self-confident not get that he was everything she wanted already? She'd well and truly been willing to give up the most important things in her life in order to be with him—and he'd made it so she didn't have to. "I love you, Levi."

She could hear the smile pushing those sexy lips in his cocky demand. "Say it again."

Pulling back so she could meet Levi's soul-deep stare, she replied, "I love you. And I want forever and everything that comes with it, *so long as I have it with you.*"

Levi caught her left hand in his, rubbing the thick pad of his thumb over the sensitive skin at the base of her fourth finger. "Forever?"

Butterflies danced through her belly as she nodded.

Then splaying a hand across the width of her abdomen, gaze steadier than his voice, he prompted again, "Forever?"

The hope and desire shining in his eyes had her heart thumping wildly in her chest. Smoothing her hand over his where it rested over her belly, she envisioned a little boy with those same perfect-day, blue-sky eyes snuggled against Levi's broad chest. "Yes."

A slow grin pushed to Levi's face. "I don't have any doubts, Elise. I love you. And I'm never going to give you up."

Pushing to her toes, she whispered against his lips, promising everything she had to give, because she knew without doubt the man who stood before her was going to spend the rest of his life doing the same. "Forever."

EPILOGUE

ELISE squinted into the morning sun, watching as Levi cut across the dew-covered field, already twenty yards ahead. If she'd had more energy she might have caught up with him, but chasing a man bent on his own purpose simply wasn't worth the exertion.

She'd tried to talk reason…but Levi wouldn't listen.

Closing in on a cluster of activity, he raised a hand in greeting, calling out to the man almost as tall as he was.

"Nate."

"Hey, man. Thought you were leaving town this week for that opening in Dallas."

Some sort of masculine hand-slapping, knuckle-bumping ritual ensued and Elise chuckled at the easy exchange.

"Nah, sent my VP instead," he answered, shooting a backward glance her way, his grin stretched so wide she wondered how it didn't break. "He plays better with the press. Besides…"

He turned, eyes holding with hers.

She knew what he was working up to. Even though she'd suggested he try to wait this time…*he just couldn't seem to stop himself.*

It was one of her favorite flaws.

Levi's already impossibly wide shoulders expanded with his held breath.

God, she wondered if she'd ever get tired of watching him. Not likely.

And then he was digging in his jeans pocket, and suddenly it was *her* breath that caught.

No. He didn't. He wouldn't. *Not again.*

The soft padded squeeze of the small hand in hers drew her attention down to the wide perfect-day, blue-sky eyes blinking up at her. "Mommy, why's Daddy's wavin' the baby stick at Coach Evans?"

Elise's lips twitched. "It's just Daddy…excited."

Excited. Elated. And apparently out of his head as well. Just as he'd been finding out about Marissa. Danny. And then Danny actually being Danny *and* Dane. Only she'd thought they'd agreed he'd stop dragging the pregnancy tests out for show-and-tell.

Nate's eyes went wide as, laughing, he took a quick step back, hands coming up to cradle the little bundle of boy, strapped securely into his baby sling. But then just as quickly, he dodged the test stick, the "Levi Davis Productions" diaper-duffel, and the double stroller with the twins Levi had been pushing—and caught her husband in a genuine, back-clapping, one-armed hug.

Another curly-lashed blink, and then their five-year-old daughter, Marissa, burst into a grin that matched her daddy's, staring after Levi with unabashed little-girl worship. "He gets *really* excited."

Elise nodded, her throat going tight with emotion as she gazed across at the best rule she'd ever broken. "About us he does."

Heading over to the sidelines, she spread a blanket. Returned a wave from Nate's wife Payton, who had been summoned to center field. After duly inspecting and admiring the pregnancy test, she jogged over to Elise, eyes still watering from her laughter.

"Congratulations," she said, offering a tight squeeze before stepping back and pulling a mock frown. "Only you do realize that Nate's going to be begging me for another baby after this."

Elise chuckled, knowing it was true. Between Nate and Levi, she didn't know which of the guys was a bigger family man. And Nate, like Levi, had the tenacious mentality that usually got him most anything he wanted. But then, Elise didn't imagine there'd really be all that much begging required, as Payton had been hinting about wanting "just one more" since their youngest was born six months earlier.

The women caught up for a few more minutes, watching as seven-year-old Ian, Nate and Payton's oldest, showed off his latest soccer moves for Marissa.

"Elise, I bet your mom's over the moon."

"Would you believe I barely got to talk to her? Levi let me get about two sentences out before he was bouncing around on the balls of his feet. It was so funny I just handed the phone over and let him detail out all the ways he'd come to suspect I was pregnant again."

Hand over her mouth, Payton shook her head. "I can only imagine."

Elise rolled her eyes. "Don't. The words 'Too much information' don't even begin to cover it. Anyway, Mom's coming over after her 'Fit at Fifty' class and then we're going to see my dad. We'll get a good chance to talk then."

Though her father wouldn't recognize either of them, or even understand what they were talking about, sharing her excitement with him was important to Elise. She knew he enjoyed the company from the way his eyes lit up when he heard the chatter of conversation, or bubble of laughter around him. And at this point that was enough.

Nate blew his whistle and Payton excused herself to

take their youngest, while Levi crouched down, absorbing the full-bodied fling of his daughter into his arms as she readied for the game.

No, Elise imagined she wouldn't ever get tired of looking at that.

Levi squeezed his little girl and wished her luck.

"I'm going to score a goal for you, Daddy," came Marissa's breathy little voice at his ear, followed by one of those whisper-soft kisses he'd never get enough of. He wondered for about the six-thousandth time in the last four hours whether this baby would be another boy or girl.

Girls were something else.

But then a peek at Dane, sleeping snuggled around that stuffed hammer he dragged everywhere, and Danny's little mop of auburn curls catching in the warm breeze—and he thought boys were pretty spectacular too. Even if they were harder to round up than a Great Dane on the loose when they put their minds to it.

Marissa left his arms, and jogged over to the other little girls, falling in with Whitney Evans as she had been from about the first minute they'd met. Whispers were exchanged and then a hug as the miniature version of Payton delightedly looked to her father and then over to him.

Her little rosebud lips formed the word, "Baby?"

Levi proudly held up the white stick as evidence before pushing the double stroller over to Elise.

He shouldn't gloat, but, feeling totally triumphant over smuggling the test out of the house, he couldn't quite help it. "I *told* you they'd want to see it."

His gorgeous wife nodded, that eternally patient smile she saved for him and the kids turning into the smile she saved just for him as he ducked down to kiss her head, then settled onto the blanket beside her.

Elise's fingers sifted through his hair, and his eyes drifted closed in momentary bliss—only to open again at the unmistakable tug of one of Marissa's barrettes coming loose.

"Butterfly?" he asked, checking the boys in their stroller.

"Glitter pony," Elise answered, handing it over so he could add it to the small collection growing in his pocket. Marissa was into doing hair in no small way.

Seeing they were still sleeping, he scooted behind Elise so her back rested against his chest and his legs bracketed hers.

"How you doing?" he asked, rubbing his cheek against the top of her head.

"A little tired, is all."

He dropped a kiss at her temple, tightening his arms. "Just lean on me for a while. I've got you."

Settling back into his hold, Elise let out a contented sigh that did all the right things to that place inside him she'd helped him fill.

Marissa's little legs kicked hard as she outran the pack and then sent the ball sailing over the goal. It was offside and way off-mark but she hadn't quite gotten that concept yet and proceeded to bounce around squealing with victorious delight.

It didn't get any better than this.

After a moment, Elise smoothed her hand over his, guiding it to rest low on her belly. "Seems early to be this wiped out, huh?"

"I was thinking that, too." He'd actually tried to convince her to stay home and rest while she had the chance— but she wouldn't hear it, and far be it from him to hold her back.

Then, threading their fingers together, she added, "Just like with the twins."

Levi grinned. Had he thought it couldn't get any better? It definitely could.

* * * * *

COMING NEXT MONTH from Harlequin Presents® EXTRA
AVAILABLE SEPTEMBER 4, 2012

#213 GIANNI'S PRIDE

Protecting His Legacy

Kim Lawrence

Can Gianni conquer his pride and admit that he might have met his match in utterly gorgeous Miranda?

#214 THE SECRET SINCLAIR

Protecting His Legacy

Cathy Williams

One spectacular night under Raoul's skilful touch leads to consequences Sarah could never have imagined: she's pregnant with the Sinclair heir!

#215 WHAT HAPPENS IN VEGAS...

Inconveniently Wed!

Kimberly Lang

Evie's scandalous baby bombshell will provide tantalising gossip-column fodder, unless she marries the dangerously attractive billionaire Nick Rocco...father of her baby!

#216 MARRYING THE ENEMY

Inconveniently Wed!

Nicola Marsh

Ruby finds herself propositioning tycoon Jax Maroney in order to save her family's company—but it's only a marriage on paper...isn't it?

You can find more information on upcoming Harlequin®
titles, free excerpts and more at www.Harlequin.com.

HPECNM0812

COMING NEXT MONTH from Harlequin Presents®
AVAILABLE AUGUST 21, 2012

#3083 CONTRACT WITH CONSEQUENCES
Miranda Lee
Scarlet wants a baby, but ruthless John Mitchell's help comes with a devilish price—that they do it the old-fashioned way!

#3084 DEFYING THE PRINCE
The Santina Crown
Sarah Morgan
Scandalized singer Izzy Jackson is whisked away from the baying press by Prince Matteo...straight from the limelight into the fire....

#3085 TO LOVE, HONOR AND BETRAY
Jennie Lucas
Callie never imagined that on her wedding day she would be kidnapped by her boss, Eduardo Cruz—the father of her unborn baby.

#3086 ENEMIES AT THE ALTAR
The Outrageous Sisters
Melanie Milburne
Sienna Baker is the last woman Andreas Ferrante would ever marry. But now she's the key to his inheritance!

#3087 DUTY AND THE BEAST
Desert Brothers
Trish Morey
Princess Aisha is rescued from the clutches of a lascivious prince by barbarian Zoltan. Now he must marry Aisha to ensure he's crowned king.

#3088 A TAINTED BEAUTY
What His Money Can't Buy
Sharon Kendrick
Ciro D'Angelo discovers his "perfect wife" isn't as pure as he'd thought! Yet once you're a D'Angelo wife—there's no escape....

You can find more information on upcoming Harlequin®
titles, free excerpts and more at www.Harlequin.com.

HPCNM0812

REQUEST YOUR FREE BOOKS!

Harlequin *Presents*

2 FREE NOVELS PLUS
2 FREE GIFTS!

PASSION GUARANTEED SEDUCTION

YES! Please send me 2 FREE Harlequin Presents® novels and my 2 FREE gifts (gifts are worth about $10). After receiving them, if I don't wish to receive any more books, I can return the shipping statement marked "cancel." If I don't cancel, I will receive 6 brand-new novels every month and be billed just $4.30 per book in the U.S. or $4.99 per book in Canada. That's a saving of at least 14% off the cover price! It's quite a bargain! Shipping and handling is just 50¢ per book in the U.S. and 75¢ per book in Canada.* I understand that accepting the 2 free books and gifts places me under no obligation to buy anything. I can always return a shipment and cancel at any time. Even if I never buy another book, the two free books and gifts are mine to keep forever.

106/306 HDN FERQ

Name _____ (PLEASE PRINT) _____

Address _____ Apt. #

City _____ State/Prov. _____ Zip/Postal Code

Signature (if under 18, a parent or guardian must sign)

Mail to the **Reader Service:**
IN U.S.A.: P.O. Box 1867, Buffalo, NY 14240-1867
IN CANADA: P.O. Box 609, Fort Erie, Ontario L2A 5X3

Not valid for current subscribers to Harlequin Presents books.

**Are you a current subscriber to Harlequin Presents books
and want to receive the larger-print edition?
Call 1-800-873-8635 or visit www.ReaderService.com.**

* Terms and prices subject to change without notice. Prices do not include applicable taxes. Sales tax applicable in N.Y. Canadian residents will be charged applicable taxes. Offer not valid in Quebec. This offer is limited to one order per household. All orders subject to credit approval. Credit or debit balances in a customer's account(s) may be offset by any other outstanding balance owed by or to the customer. Please allow 4 to 6 weeks for delivery. Offer available while quantities last.

Your Privacy—The Reader Service is committed to protecting your privacy. Our Privacy Policy is available online at www.ReaderService.com or upon request from the Reader Service.

We make a portion of our mailing list available to reputable third parties that offer products we believe may interest you. If you prefer that we not exchange your name with third parties, or if you wish to clarify or modify your communication preferences, please visit us at www.ReaderService.com/consumerschoice or write to us at Reader Service Preference Service, P.O. Box 9062, Buffalo, NY 14269. Include your complete name and address.

HP11B

HARLEQUIN *Presents*

The scandal continues in The Santina Crown miniseries with *USA TODAY* bestselling author

Sarah Morgan

Second in line to the throne, Matteo Santina knows a thing or two about keeping his cool under pressure. But when pop star singer Izzy Jackson shows up to her sister's wedding and makes a scandalous scene that goes against all royal protocol, Matteo whisks her offstage, into his limo and straight to his luxury palazzo…. Rumor has it that they have yet to emerge!

DEFYING THE PRINCE

Available August 21 wherever books are sold!

HP13090

Harlequin

SPECIAL EDITION

Life, Love and Family

Withdrawn